Praise for *The Christmas Clock*

"The perfect stocking stuffer for the romance reader on your holiday list."
> —Kristin Hannah, *New York Times* bestselling author of
> *True Colors*

"Kat Martin has given readers the perfect holiday gift. *The Christmas Clock* is a lovely tale of finding family, love, joy, and forgiveness all in one sweet package. I loved it."
> —Jill Marie Landis, bestselling author of
> *Heart of Stone*

"Charming and romantic. . . . A must read. . . ."
> —*Library Journal*, starred review

"Get your hankie ready before you settle in for Martin's novella of love and forgiveness. The sweet story is well wrought."
> —*Romantic Times*

"*The Christmas Clock* is an emotion-packed contemporary romance that will have you smiling one moment and in tears the next . . . a perfect holiday story!"
> —RomanceJunkies.com

the CHRISTMAS CLOCK

the
CHRISTMAS
*C*LOCK

A Novel

KAT MARTIN

Vanguard Press
A Member of the Perseus Books Group

Published by Vanguard Press
A Member of the Perseus Books Group

Designed by Pauline Brown
Set in 12-point Centaur MT

Cataloging-in-Publication data for this book is available from the Library of
Congress.
HC ISBN: 978-1-59315-547-6
Mass Market ISBN: 978-1-59315-593-3

Vanguard Press books are available at special discounts for bulk purchases in
the U.S. by corporations, institutions, and other organizations. For more information, please contact the Special Markets Department at the Perseus Books
Group, 2300 Chestnut Street, Suite 200, Philadelphia, PA 19103, or call
(800) 810-4145, ext. 5000, or e-mail special.markets@perseusbooks.com.

10 9 8 7 6 5 4 3 2 1

To the people of the Heartland,
for your solid values, honesty, courage,
integrity, and your strong sense of
community, God, and country.
You represent the best of America.

Christmas sings to the aged, to those who wish to hear it.
The song fills the hollows left by faded dreams, lost youth, and the
pain of missing loved ones, gone before their time.

The young hear it, too. The melody whispers promises of
what might be, of golden dreams, of a future brighter than the
present in which they live.

This is a Christmas story, a tale that changed
the lives of the people who lived it. It's a story of miracles that
might have been . . . or yet could be.

Prologue

◇◇◇◇◇◇◇◇◇◇◇◇◇◇◇◇◇◇◇◇◇◇◇

There are years in our lives that change us, mold us forever in some way. I was eight years old that Christmas, too young to really understand all the undercurrents swirling around me.

It is only now, fourteen years later, as I graduate from Michigan State University and prepare for a job in the health care industry, that I am able to look back with the clarity to see that Christmas for the miracle it truly was.

Back then, during that summer of 1994, with the trees leafed out and the sun warming my shoulders through a T-shirt that hung down to my knees, I didn't realize disaster lay just a few months ahead. I only knew I wanted to buy the beautiful clock in the window of Tremont's Antiques as a gift for my grandmother, Lottie Sparks.

I didn't know that in trying to buy the clock, I would meet the people who would change my world, and my life would never be the same.

the
CHRISTMAS
*C*LOCK

CHAPTER ONE
August 1994

◇◇◇◇◇◇◇◇

*S*ylvia Winters was going home. She had only been back to the small Michigan town of Dreyerville once in the past eight years. Her mother's funeral had demanded a return, but she had left the following day. Only a few close friends had attended the brief, graveside service held at the Greenhaven Cemetery. Marsha Winters had started drinking the day her husband disappeared. Abandoned with a

month-old baby in a ramshackle house at the edge
of town, she took up the bottle and didn't put it
down for twenty years. Neither she nor Syl ever saw
Syl's father again.

Times had been hard back then, but the years Syl
had spent in the charming rural community sur-
rounded by forested, rolling hills held memories she
cherished. She was a good student, and she was popu-
lar. In high school, a glowing future spread out before
her: a scholarship to college and a career in nursing, a
husband and children, the sort of life Syl had always
dreamed of and never had.

But life was never predictable, she had learned,
and oftentimes cruel. At nineteen, during her first
year at Dreyerville Community College, Syl had
fallen in love. She and Joe Dixon, the school's star
quarterback, were engaged to be married the summer of the following year. Syl couldn't imagine ever
being happier.

Then her world came crashing down around
her, and all of her dreams along with it. A routine
doctor's appointment had brought news so grim
that the week before the ceremony, Syl called off the
wedding. She packed her belongings that same afternoon and left for Chicago.

If it hadn't been for her mother's sister, Bessie, Syl wasn't sure she would have made it. Aunt Bess and Syl's dearest friend, Mary McGinnis Webster, had been responsible for getting her through the most difficult time of her life.

But things were different now.

Syl studied the double yellow line in the middle of the two-lane highway leading into Dreyerville. The air conditioner hummed inside the car, while outside, the temperature was hot and a little humid this late in the summer. Dense growths of leafy green trees lined both sides of the road, and a narrow stream wove its way through the grasses, bubbling and frothing in places, lazy and meandering in others.

As she drove her newly washed white Honda Civic toward the turn onto Main Street, a feeling of homecoming expanded in her chest. She recognized Barnett's Feed and Seed, just down the road from Murdock's Auto Repair at the edge of town.

Making a left onto Main, she spotted the old domed courthouse built in 1910 and the ornate clock tower in the middle of the grassy town square. A little farther down the street, Culver's Dry Cleaning held the middle spot in the long, two-story brick building that filled the block on the left, and there was Tremont's Antiques, right next to Brenner's Bakery.

Sylvia smiled. The apartment she had just rented sat above the garage at Doris Culver's house. Doris worked at Brenner's Bakery, had for years. The middle-aged woman was practically a fixture behind the counter of the shop.

Syl's friend Mary had found her the apartment. A job as a nurse in a local doctor's office had recently appeared in the employment section of the Dreyerville *Morning News*, and Mary had convinced her to send in an application. After flying out for an interview, Sylvia had gotten the job.

She was coming home at last. She wasn't sure what sort of life she could make for herself in the town she once had fled, but something told her coming back was the only way she could conquer the demons that had haunted her for the past eight years.

✳ ✳ ✳

Doris Culver didn't believe in happily ever after. She hadn't since she was nineteen, madly in love, and found her boyfriend, Ronnie Munns, in the backseat of his parent's '55 Chevy with Martha Gladstone, the local librarian. Love, Doris believed after that, was for fools and dreamers, and she never allowed herself to succumb to its lure again.

At fifty-six, Doris Culver felt old, but then she had for most of her life. Her husband, Floyd, the retired owner of Culver's Dry Cleaning, was a nondescript, balding man who wore horn-rimmed glasses and built birdhouses to fill up his empty days. Floyd was six years older than Doris, whom he had met when she came into his store with an armload of laundry. After cleaning her clothes for nearly five years, Floyd asked Doris out on a date. This July fifth, they had celebrated twenty-two years of marriage.

Doris felt as if it were fifty.

She rarely saw her husband except at dinner, which he ate mostly in silence. Afterward, he returned to his woodshop in the garage at the back of the house, where he stayed until he trudged up to bed at exactly nine P.M.

Though the sale of Floyd's business three years ago had provided them with a comfortable living, Doris had kept her job at the bakery, where she had been employed for years. She loved her job, especially decorating the cakes and cookies the shop made for holidays and other special occasions. With little else to fill her time, she went to work early and usually stayed past closing. Afterward, she returned to her two-bedroom, white stucco house on Maple Street, cooked Floyd's dinner, cleared the dishes, and spent the rest of the evening painting ceramics.

It was a consuming hobby. Every table, every bookshelf, even the window sills, held miniature clowns, birds, horses, dogs, cats, vases, and pitchers all done in the bright colors Doris used in an effort to cheer up her lonely world. Instead, somehow the crowded rows of objects, often in need of dusting, only made the house more oppressive.

Doris was glad for the hours she spent at the bakery, where the fragrant aroma of chocolate-chip cookies and fresh-baked bread was enough to buoy her spirits. The shop on Main next to Tremont's Antiques was a narrow brick building with big picture windows painted with the name Brenner's Bakery in wide, sculpted gold letters. Frank Brenner had died sixteen years ago, but the bakery, now owned by his son, remained a landmark in Dreyerville.

It was Saturday morning. Doris stood behind

the counter wiping crumbs off the top when the bell chimed above the door, indicating the arrival of a customer. She tucked a strand of gray hair dyed blond under her pink and white cap and smiled at her next-door neighbor and her grandson, Lottie and Teddy Sparks, as they walked into the shop.

"Good morning," Doris beamed. "How are you and Teddy today?"

Lottie set her shopping bag down on a little iron chair. "Darned arthritis has been acting up some, but aside from that, both of us are fine." She looked down with affection at her grandson. "We're kind of hungry, though." Lottie was wrinkled and slightly stoop-shouldered and her hair was as white as paper. Still, there was always a sparkle in her eyes and the hint of rose in her cheeks.

Doris smiled. "Well, we can certainly take care of that." She turned toward the dark-haired, fair-skinned boy, who looked up at her with big brown, soulful eyes. "So what's it going to be, Teddy? A glazed or a maple bar?" It was a Saturday morning tradition. Doris always looked forward to seeing Lottie, who had once been her fifth-grade teacher.

The pair lived in the yellow and white wood-framed house on Maple Street next door to Doris, but they didn't get to visit much, not with the hours Doris worked. But she had always admired Lottie Sparks, and Teddy was purely a treasure.

The child stared into the case that was filled with donuts: jelly, chocolate frosted with walnuts, powdered, and crumb. There were also bear claws and all manner of coffee cake rings. He nibbled his lower lip, then pointed toward the top shelf of the case.

"A maple bar, please."

"My, that does sound good." Doris plucked a piece of waxed paper from the box on the counter, reached into the case, and drew out a fat, maple-frosted bar. "Here you go, Teddy."

The little boy grinned. "Thank you, Mrs. Culver."

Lottie ordered a cinnamon roll, and Doris handed it over on another sheet of waxed paper. When Lottie turned to leave, Doris reminded her that she had forgotten to pay for her purchase.

"Silly of me." Lottie reached into her handbag for the little plastic coin purse she always carried. She asked again how much she owed, then dug through the money to find the right change, fumbling with this coin and that until she finally put the money up on the counter and Doris picked out the sum she needed.

Doris watched the woman cross the room, feeling a hint of concern. Lottie was getting more and more forgetful. Doris couldn't help wondering what would happen to Teddy if the old woman's memory continued to get worse.

The pair sat down at one of the small, round tables in front of the window to savor their purchases, and Doris watched with only a small twinge of jealousy as the boy looked up and smiled so sweetly at his grandmother.

When Doris had married Floyd at thirty-four, she was already too old to have a child, or at least she had thought so at the time. Floyd, whose two boys by a previous marriage were living with their mother in Florida, didn't really care. Occasionally, Doris wondered if, all those years ago, she had made the right decision, but deep down she knew that she was never cut out to raise a child.

Grandmother and grandson finished their treats and got up from the little round table. Doris waved good-bye as they tossed their used waxed paper and napkins into the trash can and walked out the door. She thought of Teddy and the mother he had lost

four years ago, the reason he now lived with Lottie.
If he lost his grandmother as well . . .

She shook her head, worried what the boy's future might hold.

＊ ＊ ＊

Lottie exchanged places with her grandson on the
sidewalk, positioning herself between him and the
light passage of Dreyerville traffic on Main Street.
At seventy-one, Lottie never would have suspected
she would be raising an eight-year-old boy, though it
shouldn't have surprised her.

Her only daughter, Wilma, had never been the
responsible sort. In her early teens, Wilma had run
away from home more than once. She missed school,
and started smoking in secret when she was fourteen. Lottie found her drunk the first time two years
later. The girl had graduated high school by the
sheer force of Lottie's will, though she never went
on to college as Lottie had hoped.

Instead, at the age of thirty-seven, after two failed
marriages and a string of deadbeat, live-in boyfriends,
Wilma had wound up pregnant by the married man
she was dating. Four years later, after drinking and par-
tying with a friend, she had lost control of her car on
her way home and died when she hit a tree.

Lottie had wound up with Teddy, but he wasn't a burden. The boy had become the joy of her life.

As they walked along the sidewalk, she felt his small hand in hers and smiled. Glancing ahead, her steps began to slow and Teddy came to a halt beside her. Both of them looked into the window of Tremont's Antiques, a favorite place to visit on their Saturday morning outings. Today, they didn't go in, but Lottie could see the small Victorian hand-painted clock she had been admiring for nearly a year.

"It's still there, Gramma."

"Yes, I see it is." Lottie loved clocks. She owned four beautiful antique clocks she had purchased over the years and a big grandfather clock her late husband, Chester, had bought for her on their fortieth wedding anniversary.

But this little clock was special. It reminded her of the one her mother had on the wall in the kitchen when she was a little girl. She used to sit at the old oak table and watch the hands move over the face while her mother baked cookies. The clock at Tremont's reminded her of the happy days of her childhood, memories that were rapidly fading.

Lottie's chest tightened with sudden despair. Something terrible was happening to her, something she couldn't fight and simply could not stop.

Two years ago, she had been diagnosed with Alzheimer's disease. At first the signs were subtle: misplacing objects, forgetting the date right after she had looked at the calendar, not remembering little words like *cat* or *comb*, saying another word in its place. Worried, she had gone to see her longtime family physician, Dr. Waller. He had referred her to a doctor named Davis, who specialized in Alzheimer's cases.

Several visits that included a medical history of her family, a physical examination, a brain scan, and a mental status evaluation revealed the truth. She had a very progressive form of Alzheimer's, a type of dementia that destroyed brain cells and robbed the mind of memory. She could expect the symptoms to worsen at a very rapid pace, and she needed to be prepared. Eventually, the disease would kill her.

Lottie looked down at Teddy, who was staring up at her with big, worried, brown eyes.

"Gramma? Are you all right?"

How long had she been standing there? She had no idea. She managed a smile for Teddy. "I'm fine, sweetheart. Why don't we go on home?"

Teddy looked relieved. Lottie gazed off down

the street, which suddenly seemed less familiar. Their house was located two blocks farther down Main, then left on Maple Street. So far, she hadn't forgotten how to get there, but the doctors had warned her it could happen.

Teddy took her hand as they started walking. She let him lead the way. She wondered if he had noticed the subtle changes coming over her, and she suspected that he had. Lottie was a deeply religious woman. She was ready to meet her maker, though she would have preferred another path to glory. She would go without complaint, but there was Teddy to consider.

Her husband had passed away eight years ago. Her sister and daughter were dead. She had some distant cousins, but they were more feeble than she and certainly not suitable parents for an eight-year-old boy. For the past two years, ever since she had learned of her condition, Lottie had been hoping to find an answer to the problem of Teddy's future.

Before it was too late, she had to find Teddy a home.

CHAPTER TWO

◇◇◇◇◇◇◇◇◇◇◇◇◇◇◇◇◇◇◇◇

*S*yl was supposed to meet Mrs. Culver at one o'clock on Saturday to get a key to her new apartment. Arriving a little early, she drove around for a while, enjoying the feeling of homecoming, grateful that few changes had been made in the little town she since had moved away.

At a few minutes before one, she pulled up in front of the house on Maple Street. Driving a Volvo station wagon, Doris Culver pulled in right behind her. Syl watched her climb out of her car, thinking the woman looked exactly the way Syl remembered but thinner and paler, her gray-blond hair a little wispier.

"Welcome back," Mrs. Culver said, handing her the key. "I hope you like the place all right."

Syl smiled. "It'll be all mine. That's a first for me—which means I'm sure to like it."

Mrs. Culver insisted she call her Doris and also insisted on helping carry Syl's belongings up to her newly acquired quarters above the garage.

"You can do whatever you want with it," Doris said as they climbed the stairs. "Make it feel like it's your own."

"Thank you."

"You don't have any pets, do you?"

She had never had a pet. Why did it suddenly seem as if she had missed something? "I'm afraid not."

One of Doris's blond eyebrows went up. "Well, small animals are okay, if you decide to get one."

Syl smiled, liking the notion. "Maybe I will."

Doris started back down the stairs to her house, a gray wood-framed home built in the thirties, then stopped and turned.

"Tomorrow's Sunday. I go to the Presbyterian

Church over on Elm. Maybe you'd like to come with me."

Syl hadn't been to church since she had left Dreyerville. Why not, she thought. She was making a new beginning. Maybe starting back to church was a good idea.

"Thank you, I'd like that very much."

"Service starts at eleven."

Syl just nodded. Already her life was changing. Or perhaps it was only changing back.

A shiver ran through her. When she had left Dreyerville, she'd been engaged to Joe Dixon. Four years ago, Mary had written to tell her that Joe had moved back to town. Syl knew he had spent the previous three years in prison. She also knew that she was the cause.

Her stomach tightened. Sooner or later, she was bound to run into him. She had no idea what he might say to her or what she might say to him, but maybe facing Joe was part of the reason she had come back.

At least their meeting wouldn't be today and, with luck, probably not tomorrow, since Joe wasn't much of a church-goer, or at least he hadn't been, back then.

With her car unloaded, she closed the apartment

door behind her and turned to survey her domain: living room, kitchen with eating area, two bedrooms, and a bath, more than enough room for her. The place was furnished, which was good, because she had been living with her aunt and didn't own much except for her clothes and a few treasured personal possessions.

When she had first arrived in Chicago, she had stayed with Aunt Bess because she needed her aunt's help and support. Two years ago, the tables had turned and it was Bess who needed her. She had suffered a debilitating stroke; then six months ago, the woman who'd been far more a mother than Syl's own, had died at the age of fifty-two.

That was when Syl began thinking of home, imagining what it might be like to return. Then Mary had phoned, and now she was here.

* * *

Doris usually went to church by herself. Each week, she asked Floyd to go with her, but there was always something more important he had to do.

They used to go together each week, but over the years, Floyd accompanied her less and less. Today, she left him working, boring a hole in the front of one of the little wooden birdhouses he built out in his shop behind the house. Floyd sold them down at Barnett's Feed and Seed, the local mercantile, and a couple of other places in town, more to feel useful in his retirement than for the extra income he earned.

Dressed in her favorite pink linen suit, Doris waited at the bottom of the stairs leading up to the apartment she had rented to Sylvia Winters, and a few minutes later, the girl came hurrying down the steps. She was smaller than Doris, about five feet four, and pretty, with short, honey-brown hair that curled softly around her face, and light green eyes.

"I hope I'm not late."

"I'm a little early. Are you ready?"

"I sure am."

They got into Doris's station wagon and drove over to the Presbyterian Church. It was humid, the sun heating the air and dampness seeping into Doris's clothes. A small crowd gathered near the door, forming a circle around the minister, the Reverend Thomas Gains, who stood on the steps of the white wooden building with its tall white steeple. Lottie parked the car, and she and Sylvia walked over to join the group.

"Good morning, Doris," Reverend Gains welcomed her. "I see you've brought a friend."

"I'm Sylvia Winters. I just moved back to town." Sylvia held out a slim hand, and the reverend shook it.

"It's nice to meet you. I hope we'll see you often."

He turned back to Doris. "How is Floyd?" The minister always asked this question, and it always embarrassed her.

"He's fine. Had a bit of a headache this morning. I'll give him your regards."

"Please do."

She thought of Floyd at work in his dusty shop and cast a glance at Sylvia. They made their way inside the church.

* * *

Mondays were always busy. Joe Dixon wiped his hands on an old grease rag and tossed it up on the shelf. All three bays at Murdock's Auto Repair were full of cars, and there were several more waiting outside. Murdock's was the best garage for miles around, and people lined up for service.

Joe smiled at the thought. Being a mechanic was a dirty, greasy, noisy job, and he loved every minute of it. Since he'd been a sophomore in high school, he had dabbled with cars. In his senior year, he had run across an old '66 Chevy Super Sport headed for the junkyard, bought it for a song, and overhauled it with his dad's help, turning it into the big red muscle car it was back in its day.

He'd worked two jobs that summer to pay for the parts he needed, most of which came from the junk yard meant to be the car's final resting spot.

That success had pointed him toward a career in auto mechanics. He had known even then he wanted to own his own shop, and now, at twenty-nine, he was finally on the way to making it happen. In the four years since his return to Dreyerville, he had become half owner of Murdock's garage. He would own the whole business by the time Bumper Murdock was ready to retire.

The phone rang and Joe walked over and picked up the receiver. It was Mrs. Murphy, one of his customers.

"Joe, I can't get my car started," she said. "I think the battery is dead. I'm supposed to be at choir practice in half an hour. What should I do?"

"I've got to finish checking the oil for a guy in the waiting room, then I'll come on over. I'll give you a ride to church and then take car of your car."

A sigh of relief whispered over the phone. "Thanks, Joe."

He smiled. "See you in a couple of minutes."

Hurrying toward the sporty little yellow convertible that belonged to Jim Higgins, one of the male nurses at the hospital, he checked the oil, and added a quart.

"How much do I owe you?" Jim asked.

"Just the price of the oil."

"Great. Thanks, Joe."

"Glad to help."

Thinking of Mrs. Murphy as he strode toward his truck, he glanced around the shop. If things had been different, he would already have owned the business. He wouldn't have wasted three years of his life in the state penitentiary.

Or in fairness, maybe he would have wound up there, anyway. He'd been a hothead back then, as good with his fists as he was with his hands when he worked on a car.

Still, it was Syl's disappearance that had set events in motion.

A muscle clenched in his jaw. Sylvia Winters, the woman he had loved, had nearly destroyed his life.

✳   ✳   ✳

It was Monday. Lottie knew because the repair shop called to remind her of her appointment. After making sure Teddy fastened his seatbelt, Lottie backed the car into the alley behind the house. It was a 1984 Mercury Topaz that Chester had purchased two years before he died. She didn't drive it much, only to the doctor's office or to King's Supermarket or, as today, to the repair shop.

Chester had always taken the car to Murdock's Auto Repair on Main at the edge of town, so she went there, too. A nice young man named Joe Dixon did most of the work there now, and he seemed to be honest, never overcharging, always finishing the work on schedule.

Lottie couldn't remember for sure if she had called Joe on Friday or another day in the week, but this morning she had found the note she had placed beneath the red plastic magnet on her refrigerator, reminding her of her ten o'clock appointment to have the oil changed. It was summer vacation, so Teddy was home from school and Lottie was enjoying his company.

Still, the confused state she often found herself in was occurring more and more often, and she didn't like the idea of Teddy seeing her that way. Concentrating on the road, Lottie saw the repair shop on the right-hand side, signaled, and pulled into a parking space in front of the building.

✳ ✳ ✳

Joe Dixon spotted the faded blue metallic Mercury at the same time Bumper Murdock called out the news.

"Mrs. Sparks is here." Bumper checked off the appointment on his clipboard. "Which bay do you want her in?"

Joe waved to the little white-haired woman barely visible behind the wheel of her car. He had been taking care of Lottie Sparks's auto for years. The Merc was in tip-top condition. It was its owner who had started to fade.

"The middle bay is good," Joe said, waiting while Bumper gave directions for Lottie to line up the car and drive it onto the lift. Her grandson was with her, Joe saw, remembering that school was out for the summer. The little boy must be seven or eight, dark hair, dark eyes, cute little guy, smart as a whip. Joe had always loved children, boys or girls, it didn't really matter.

Being a stone's throw from thirty, he had imagined himself married by now and raising a passel of kids. Instead, he was single, a loner who rarely dated or even went out. Joe frowned as memories of Syl and him began to pour in. He shoved them back into a corner and went over to speak to Lottie Sparks.

He was working on the Mercury twenty minutes later, Lottie in the waiting room sipping a cup of coffee, when little Teddy wandered into the service area. The kid's neck swiveled around as he took in the grease guns, tool boards, tire changers, and air guns. His brown eyes fixed on Bumper, who was working on a Toyota, the left rear wheel jacked into the air while Bumper used the air gun to remove the nuts from the wheel.

The kid stood unmoving, transfixed by the loud buzzing sounds and how easily the wheel came off. Bumper rolled the tire over to the changer, and Teddy's gaze moved off in another direction.

"What kinda car is that?" He pointed toward Joe's prize possession, a black and white '64 Thunderbird convertible, a big four-seater with long, sleek fins. Joe only drove it once in a while, but he had really enjoyed fixing it up.

"That's a T-bird, son. They don't make 'em like that anymore."

"Can I see inside?"

Joe flicked a glance at Lottie, who seemed content where she sat on the brown vinyl sofa in the waiting room, and tilted his head toward the car. "Sure, why not?"

Teddy grinned and raced over. One of his eye teeth was missing, though his front two had come in, a sign that the boy was growing up.

"You get a quarter from the tooth fairy for that?" Joe asked.

Teddy looked up at him. "She came for these two." He pointed at his two front teeth. "I got fifty cents. Gramma said the fairy would come for this one, but she didn't. I guess she forgot."

More likely the tooth fairy being Lottie Sparks had forgotten. Joe had noticed that the old woman was becoming more and more forgetful.

He opened the driver's side door of the T-bird and motioned for Teddy to climb in behind the wheel.

"Wow, this is great." The kid was too small to see out, but he sat there grinning, leaning back in the red leather seat.

"Yeah, pretty great." Joe reached down and ruffled the little boy's hair. "You like cars, Teddy?"

"I love 'em. I'm gonna have a really fast car when I grow up."

Joe laughed. He could remember thinking that same thing. His second car had been a hot '82 Camaro with a custom grill and a four-speed manual transmission. Little Teddy would have loved it.

Joe smiled at the memory and helped the boy climb down from the car. "We're just about done with the Merc. Tell your grandmother it'll only be a few more minutes."

Teddy didn't move. "I was thinking . . . I been raking up leaves for Mrs. Culver—the lady in the house next door to ours. And I'm weeding for Mr. Stillwater across the street. Do you think you might have some work I could do?"

Joe shook his head. "Sorry, kid. A garage isn't a good place for someone your age. Too much heavy equipment. Too many ways you might get hurt."

The boy's face fell. He gazed around the shop like it was Disneyland and he couldn't get a ticket to get in. "I need to make some money so I can buy my gramma a present."

"Yeah? What kind of present?"

"A clock. She loves it. She always stops to look at it when we go to town. I'm saving up so I can buy it for her for Christmas."

Joe thought of the woman in the other room. From what Bumper had told him, Lottie Sparks was all the family the little boy had. Mother dead. No father. No man at all in the family.

Teddy was studying the engine Joe was working on in the corner. Joe knew it was stupid, but all of a sudden there he was, opening his mouth, probably letting himself in for trouble.

"I'll tell you what. You go ask your grandmother. If it's all right with her, you can work a couple of hours a day cleaning up around here."

Teddy grinned, flashing the hole where his tooth should have been. He turned and raced off toward the waiting room and a few minutes later, Lottie Sparks walked in.

"Teddy says you want to hire him."

"I know this isn't the best place for a kid to work, Mrs. Sparks, but I promise not to let him come in here where we keep the heavy equipment, not unless I'm with him."

"It isn't good for a boy to be around an old woman all the time. He could use a man's guidance. You just make sure he doesn't get hurt."

"I'll keep a real close eye on him, Mrs. Sparks."

"He can ride his bike down here. It's only a few blocks. Long as he goes the back way, there won't be any traffic."

"That sounds good. If he wants, he can start tomorrow afternoon."

Teddy was grinning again. "What time, Mr. Dixon?"

"How about ten till noon? And it's Joe, not Mr. Dixon. And that guy over there, that's Bumper."

"Bumper?" Teddy turned toward the stout man walking toward them. Bumper was almost twice Joe's age, looking forward to an early retirement. At five feet nine, he was five inches shorter than Joe and built like a fireplug. "That's a funny name," Teddy said.

"They started calling him that when he was a kid," Joe explained. He and Bumper's son, Charlie, were best friends, had been since they were freshmen at Dreyerville High.

"Because he liked cars?" Teddy asked.

Because, according to Charlie, he was pudgy as a kid and always running into things. But Joe just said, "Yeah, Bumper's a top mechanic."

Teddy looked up at Bumper with awe but made no comment. The man beneath the grease-stained overalls was still a little chunky, but not like the old days, at least according to Charlie.

The Merc was finished. Joe backed the car out

of the garage and waited while Mrs. Sparks and Teddy climbed in.

As he watched them drive away, he thought of all the problems a kid Teddy's age could cause, how much time watching the boy would take, and marveled at the crazy things he sometimes got himself into.

CHAPTER THREE

<hr />

*L*ottie had an appointment with Dr. Davis at three o'clock the following Monday. She hadn't remembered the time or even that she was supposed to go, but she had written it down on a piece of paper and laid it on the kitchen counter.

Lottie thought of her car, newly serviced and parked in the garage behind her house. It was a bit of a drive to the doctor's office, and she had gotten a little confused driving back the last time. She must have made the appointment for Monday because

Monday was one of Doris Culver's days off. Doris was a good friend and a very good neighbor.

Though Lottie hadn't told her about the Alzheimer's yet, she had mentioned her advancing years, her reluctance to drive, and that she was thinking of selling her car. Doris had volunteered to drive her anyplace she needed to go, and Lottie had taken her up on it.

Teddy was at work at his summer job at Murdock's Auto Repair, so she didn't have to worry about him. She climbed into Doris's car, and the station wagon pulled away from the curb.

A few minutes later, they were on their way to Dr. Davis's office on Franklin Street not far down the block from the entrance to Community Hospital. The streets of Dreyerville were lined on both sides with sycamore trees so old they grew together over the road, forming a rich, green canopy. This warm August afternoon, the sun shown down through the branches, dappling the hood of the car.

"Why don't you go ahead and get out," Doris said, "and I'll go find a parking spot." Wearing tan slacks and a beige blouse, Doris always dressed conservatively, pulling her hair back into a bun, never wearing too much makeup. She had never been particularly pretty, not even when she was a girl, but now in her fifties, there was a pinched quality to her features, a tired look around her mouth.

Doris's disappointment in life seemed to show in her face, Lottie thought. Except when she was at the bakery. There she looked more like the young, hopeful girl that she had once been.

Lottie cracked open the door. "I really appreciate this, Doris. I don't think I'll be in there very long." The office sign sat next to the door, helpfully pointing the way. Lottie walked in that direction.

The receptionist smiled and pulled out her chart, and a few minutes later, Lottie was headed for the nurses' station. With the arthritis in her hip, she couldn't walk as fast as she used to, so it took her a while to make her way down the long, narrow corridor.

One of the nurses was waiting, a slender young woman in her late twenties with tawny brown hair, light green eyes, and a pretty smile. She was new, Lottie thought, or maybe she just didn't remember her.

"Good morning . . ." Lottie read the name on the woman's badge. "Sylvia."

"Good morning, Mrs. Sparks. How are you feeling today?"

Lottie mentioned her arthritis, but both of them knew that wasn't what the nurse was asking about. The young woman took her blood pressure then led her into one of the examining rooms. Sylvia helped her get settled in a gray vinyl, metal-framed chair and quietly closed the door.

* * *

Fighting a surge of pity, Syl turned away from the aging woman she recognized as living in the house next door to her apartment. She had met her neighbor, Lottie Sparks and her grandson, Teddy, at church the morning she had gone with Doris. She hadn't expected to see the elderly woman the following week in the doctor's office, being treated for a rapidly progressing form of Alzheimer's disease.

Sylvia glanced toward the door of the examining room. Alzheimer's was eventually fatal, and Lottie's disease was moving fairly fast. Her medical records listed a cousin in New Jersey as next of kin. If the cousin wouldn't take Lottie's grandson, she hoped there was someone else who would. If not, he would go into the foster care system. She hated to think what sort of place he might wind up in.

Syl walked over to the desk in the reception area and set down a couple of files. Across the way, she spotted her landlady, Doris Culver, sitting in one of the vinyl chairs and reading a copy of *Better Homes and Gardens*. Doris had probably driven Lottie to her appointment. Sylvia walked over to say hello.

"Good morning, Doris. Are you waiting for Mrs. Sparks?"

"Why, yes, I am."

"She's in with Dr. Davis, but she shouldn't be too much longer."

Sylvia noticed the page lying open in Doris's lap, a photo of a cheerful, airy home filled with lush, green plants.

"I know it's none of my business," Doris said, "but is Lottie all right? When I drove her here two weeks ago, I thought she was coming in for a simple checkup."

"I wish I could tell you, but I can't divulge patient information. I'd get fired if I did. Why don't you ask her what's going on? She might be glad to have someone to talk to about it."

"All right, I will." Doris smiled. "In the meantime, I hope you're getting settled in."

"I'm completely unpacked. I'm looking forward to buying some plants and things to make the apartment feel more homey."

"That's a good idea. I'm very good with plants.

I think they make all the difference." Doris's look turned thoughtful. "I hope Floyd doesn't make too much noise out in his shop."

The sawing and hammering could be kind of a nuisance at times, but Mr. Culver never worked past nine in the evening and the apartment actually sat over the garage, not the shop, so it wasn't really so bad.

"I'm getting to where I hardly notice."

"That's good to hear."

"I'll check on Mrs. Sparks." Syl turned and walked away, hoping Lottie Sparks would confide in her friend. Going through Alzheimer's was difficult enough without trying to do it alone. She was certain Lottie wouldn't mention the problem to her grandson, at least not until she had to, and even then, it would be hard for him to understand.

Syl thought about the darling little boy who lived in the house next door. She had always wanted children. She and Joe had planned to have at least three or four of them.

Then the week before their wedding, she had gone in to see her family physician for a gynecological exam. She had been having some problems with her periods and wasn't sure of the cause. Testing had revealed cervical cancer, fairly well progressed. Treatment would require a complete hysterectomy, followed by chemotherapy.

Syl had been devastated. She was engaged to a man who wanted a family more than anything in the world. And there was no guarantee that the chemo would work.

Still, she knew without a doubt that if she told Joe what was happening, he would say it didn't matter. He would say that he loved her and he wanted to marry her anyway.

But depriving Joe Dixon of the family he so desperately wanted simply would not have been fair. And making a young man with a bright future deal with the possibility of losing his wife to cancer was simply unthinkable.

Instead, Syl had ended her engagement and left for Chicago. She had refused to return Joe's calls, refused to see him when he followed her to the city. She had lied to him, told him she had never really loved him and that they were both better off going their separate ways.

A broken heart, she believed, was better than a broken future.

In the years after her recovery, she had tried to

forget the man she had loved so much, tried to forget the pain she felt whenever she heard his name. Over the years, she had worked to make a new life for herself, and for the most part, she had succeeded.

But a day rarely went by that she didn't think of Joe, didn't remember the lies she had told him, the heartbreak she had caused, and that she had ruined his life.

❋ ❋ ❋

Teddy Sparks arrived at Murdock's Repair Shop about fifteen minutes early, as he had every day since he started. Neither Joe nor Bumper were in the waiting room when he got there. Teddy wandered into the shop and saw a pair of long legs in faded jeans sticking out from beneath a jacked-up car, and strolled over.

"Hi, Joe."

Joe wheeled himself out from beneath the body of the car. "Hey, kid." He checked his wristwatch. "You're early again today. I appreciate a man with enthusiasm."

Teddy grinned. He liked when Joe talked that way. Liked that Joe treated him like a grown-up. "Whatcha want me to do?"

Joe wiped his hands on a grease rag. "Come on. You can sweep up the waiting room."

As Joe rested a hand on his shoulder and began to guide him toward the waiting room, Teddy looked wistfully behind him at all the cool machinery. He'd been hoping that today might be the day he'd get to do some work in the shop, maybe use a grease gun or something. Instead, Joe handed him the same ol' broom and dustpan he had used every afternoon and pointed down at the floor.

"Let me know when you're done, and I'll find something else for you to do."

Teddy nodded, then brightened. The day wasn't over. Maybe he'd get to use the grease gun yet. "Okay, Joe."

"Take your time. You've been doing a good job so far. I don't want to see any dirt."

Teddy was going to make sure there wasn't any to see. He liked doing a good job, liked it when someone said he had. Joe Dixon had taken a chance on him, and Teddy didn't want him to regret it.

The broom felt clumsy in his hands. He fought to get a grip on the handle and set to work sweeping the floor. Joe came in a little later and moved the sofa so he could sweep underneath, then shoved it back into place.

"You can dust when you're finished," Joe said. "You remember where the dust cloth and furniture polish are?"

He nodded, pointed toward a cabinet at the far end of the room. "Up in that cupboard."

No grease gun. At least not today, but Teddy remained optimistic. He had only been working at the shop for a week, but he really liked it. Liked the noise and the smells and the laughter. It seemed like there was always something that made Joe and Bumper laugh.

And he liked working for a man who knew all about cars, the way Joe Dixon did.

❆ ❆ ❆

The trip home from the doctor's office didn't take long. Doris pulled up in front of Lottie's house and turned off the engine. All the way home, she had been trying to work up the nerve to ask Lottie what was wrong.

"Thank you, Dorie. I appreciate your taking me to . . ." The words trailed off and Lottie's silver eyebrows drew together in confusion.

"The doctor's office," Doris gently reminded her. "We went to see Dr. Davis."

"Oh, yes, of course." She reached for the handle of the door.

"Lottie . . ."

"Yes, dear?"

"What's wrong? Won't you please confide in me?"

Lottie sat back in the seat, and for an instant, her face seemed to crumple. She let out a tired, resigned sigh. "I forget things, dear. The doctor says I have . . . Alzheimer's."

"Oh, Lottie."

"It isn't that uncommon as people get older. Unfortunately, I have the sort that hits folks at a younger age and progresses fairly quickly."

"I'm so sorry."

"Yes, well, we don't get to choose our diseases. I hope you won't say anything, Dorie. Teddy's too young to really understand, and I wouldn't like to be the center of gossip."

"You know me better than that. I won't say a word."

"Thank you, dear." She cracked open the door and climbed out. For a moment, Lottie stood on the sidewalk looking at her front door. Then she turned back to Doris. "Where did you say we went?"

"To the doctor's office."

"Oh, yes, that's right. Thank you, Dorie."

"You're welcome, Lottie. Let me know if you need another ride."

Lottie just nodded, turned, and wandered off toward the house.

CHAPTER FOUR

◇◇◇◇◇◇◇◇◇◇◇◇◇◇◇◇◇◇

The late summer grew hot and the days passed slowly. The ceiling fan in the bedroom of Syl's small apartment did little to cool the humid air. The window air conditioner worked, but it was old and the apartment never really got cool. Syl didn't mind. She preferred the warmth of summer to the long, cold, snowy days of winter, except, of course, for Christmas.

Syl loved the holidays, when the streets over-flowed with shoppers searching for just the right gift, when the lampposts were decorated with wreaths and holly, and tiny multicolored Christmas lights hung in store windows and everyone seemed to have a smile.

Brenner's Bakery was a favorite place to visit that time of year. The shop overflowed with Christmas treats decorated in bright red and green, and the rich, yeasty aromas of baked goods filled the air. Though Christmas was still months away, Syl found herself looking forward to the first time she had been home for Christmas in years.

In the meantime, she was enjoying her job, the lazy weekends fixing up her apartment, and seeing old friends. She had lunch with Mary Webster at least once a week. But now with a husband and two beautiful children, Mary had less time to spend with her friend.

Syl and Doris were developing a friendship. Doris was about as old as Syl's mother would have been, and Syl was grateful for the older woman's guidance. They talked about Lottie and poor little Teddy and what was to become of him, and some-times they talked about when Syl was a girl in Dreyerville.

"I remember you coming into the bakery,"

Doris said as they sat at the small, round table in Sylvia's kitchen drinking a glass of iced tea. "Your hair was lighter back then, almost blond, and you had freckles."

"I still do," Syl said with a laugh. "Even more than I had before."

"Well, they look good on you. You're even prettier than you were when you were engaged to Joe."

A knot squeezed in Syl's stomach.

"I never understood what happened between the two of you," Doris continued. "You both seemed so much in love. The whole town used to talk about what a fairy-tale couple you were."

Syl's fingers tightened around the icy glass. "Sometimes things happen."

"Yes, I suppose they do. Look what happened to Joe after you left."

Syl stared into her drink, watched a cube of ice bobbing in the dark liquid. "I didn't know he went to prison until a year or so later. Mary knew I'd be upset. She told me he got into a bar fight down at that roadhouse near the train tracks and a man got killed."

Doris nodded. "Al's Place. Way I heard it, some fella made a remark about you, and Joe got mad. Joe had been drinking . . . started drinking real hard after you left town. He and the guy got into it pretty good. Joe punched him, and when the guy fell, he hit his head on the brass foot rail under the bar. Killed him right on the spot."

Syl's insides twisted. "I never knew the whole story. I didn't . . . didn't know Joe got into that fight because of me." She swallowed, feeling a hollow ache in the pit of her stomach. "I knew he went to prison and that eventually he got out."

"That's right. Involuntary manslaughter. He was sentenced to five years. Got out in three for good behavior and came back to Dreyerville about four years ago. He's half owner over at Murdock's garage."

"That's good. I'm glad he's doing well. I guess . . . I guess he never got married. That's what Mary said."

"For a while, he got real serious with Diane Ellison. She's a kindergarten teacher over at Dreyerville Elementary. Looked like they were going to get married, but it didn't work out." She flicked Syl a glance. "Funny . . . I guess it hasn't worked out for either one of you."

* * *

On Friday after work, Syl and Doris went grocery

shopping at King's Supermarket. As they walked
down the aisle in front of the milk counter, sharing
the same basket for the few items each of them
needed, Syl found herself thinking of the conversation they'd had about Joe and wondering if he
knew she had come back to town. Her stomach
knotted at the thought of what his response would
be if he did.

She pushed the cart down the aisle while Doris
went off to collect a pound of butter and a loaf of
bread. The store needed remodeling. The aisles were
too narrow, and the manager kept it far too cold to
suit Syl. Still, the selection was good and the meat
and vegetables always fresh.

They were just passing the mayonnaise and
pickle aisle when their cart collided with one coming around the corner from the opposite direction.
Syl looked up to see the man who hovered in her
thoughts. He was pushing a cart, his big hands
wrapped around the handle.

Joe didn't seem to notice Doris at all, just stared
straight at Syl. She could feel the blood drain from
her face, which must have turned the same color as
the jar of mayonnaise she held in her hand. When
both of them said nothing, just kept staring at
each other, Doris said something about needing a

head of lettuce for Floyd's supper and quietly slipped away.

Syl stood frozen. She had known she would run into Joe sooner or later. Still, it was a shock to find him standing right in front of her, his jaw set and his thick black eyebrows pulled together in a frown. A smile that really wasn't edged the corners of his mouth.

"Afternoon, Syl. I heard you were back in town."

She swallowed. "Hello . . . Joe."

"Kind of surprised to hear you'd come back. I didn't think you were interested in living in a small-time, one-horse town like Dreyerville."

Syl fought not to wince. It was exactly what she had said, word for word, one of the many lies she had told. She wanted to live in Chicago, she had said, where she could experience new and exciting things.

"I guess I found out life in the city isn't all it's cracked up to be."

The un-smile stayed on his face. With his hard jaw and brilliant blue eyes, how could she have forgotten how handsome he was? But then, deep down, she hadn't. She hadn't forgotten a single thing about Joe.

"You're a nurse now, I hear, working over at old Doc Davis's office."

"I work for his son, Harry." She tried for a smile but failed. Inside her chest, her heart beat a little too fast. "Doris says you're part owner of Murdock's auto shop. That's great, Joe."

Joe said nothing. She noticed his hands still curled around the handle of the cart.

"Why'd you come back, Syl?" he asked softly. "Why didn't you stay in Chicago?"

She found a bit of courage and stiffened her spine. "Dreyerville is my home, Joe. It always has been. When Aunt Bessie died, I realized this was where I wanted to be."

"I heard about your aunt. I'm sorry."

"Thank you."

His gaze ran over her, but there was only insolence in his expression, none of the softness he used to reserve just for her. "You should have stayed in the city, Syl."

"I have the same right to be here as you do, Joe."

He made no reply, but neither did he move out of her way. Another cart rolled up behind him. Joe shoved his cart a little to the right so the gray-haired man could pass, but he still blocked Syl's way. "You never got married?"

"No."

"I figured you'd marry one of those rich city boys."

"I didn't go there for that."

"No?" His mouth turned hard. "Maybe someday you'll tell me the reason you did go. What you thought you'd find in Chicago that you couldn't find right here with me." He started pushing his basket, angling it so it rolled past hers without touching it. "See ya around, Syl."

He didn't look at her again, just kept pushing the cart straight ahead. He stopped and tossed in a jar of pickles, then rounded the end of the aisle and disappeared out of sight.

As Doris walked back toward the cart, Syl released the breath she had been holding, but regret remained tight in her chest.

Doris dropped a head of lettuce into the basket. "I guess Joe was surprised to see you."

"Not really. He knew I was in town. There aren't many secrets in Dreyerville."

"Not many, but there's still a few." *Like the truth about why you left,* Doris's expression seemed to say.

Syl wished she could tell her. Before that, she

had to work up the courage to tell Joe. After what she had put him through, he deserved to hear it before anyone else.

"He's turned into a fine man," Doris said.

Syl was silent.

"After all the trouble he had, it's nice he's been able to make something of himself."

Syl felt the unexpected sting of tears. "He was supposed to finish college. I always thought he would."

"I think he likes what he's doing. He's real good at it."

"Yes, I imagine he is," she said, taking a calming breath. "Joe was always good at whatever he did."

"Maybe you should talk to him. Appears to me the two of you have left a lot unsaid."

Syl looked down the aisle where Joe's tall figure had disappeared. Doris was right. There was a whole lot left unsaid, and she would have to say it soon.

She wondered what would happen when she did.

※ ※ ※

Joe walked out of King's and got into his red '68 Mustang. It had been a rusty pile of junk when he'd bought it the year he'd come back to town. Since then, he'd put in new black leather seats, replaced the engine and the quarter panels, souped it up, and added chrome wheels. When it came to cars, he was still a kid at heart and that probably wouldn't change.

Besides, he had an old pickup parked at the shop to use when they needed to haul stuff. Joe fired up the powerful engine and threw the car into reverse. He hit the gas a little harder than he meant to and shot out of his parking space in the supermarket lot.

He'd known she was in town. Charlie had heard the news down at the café and thought he'd want to know. Sooner or later, he was bound to run into her.

He just didn't think he'd get mad.

After three years in prison, he thought he was over that kind of reaction. But the instant he had spotted her standing in the grocery aisle, he had wanted to . . . *to what?*

It wasn't Syl's fault he'd started drinking and carousing and wound up in jail. So she'd broken their engagement. It happened to guys all the time.

But Joe had never thought it would happen to him, not with Syl. And once he had lost her, he just couldn't pull himself together. He had started hanging out in the bars, drinking and getting into fist-fights. He had dropped out in his third year of college and given up the football scholarship he had won to the University of Michigan, and his friends had stopped calling. He took up with a bunch of rowdies he wouldn't have given the time of day before Syl left town.

Joe pulled the car up in front of the repair shop and turned off the engine.

Damn, she was still beautiful. He had imagined her older, with little wrinkles around her mouth and that hard, used look some city women got. At twenty-eight, Syl Winters could have starred in a movie. Well, at least any movie Joe might want to see.

Her skin was as smooth as he remembered, her hair the color of honey, a little darker now, maybe, but that short, glossy cap of curls was as fetching as ever. Her eyes were that same pretty sea green, and she still had freckles on her nose. And a knockout figure.

He felt a sexual stirring he hadn't expected and clenched his jaw, refusing to allow his thoughts to slide in that direction. But he couldn't help remembering that night by the lake just two weeks before their wedding. He'd made love to Syl Winters, and though he had been with other women over the years, he had never truly made love to any other woman since.

Not that he hadn't tried.

For nearly a year, he had dated Diane Ellison, a local kindergarten teacher, but in the end, both of them realized it wasn't going to work. After they had ended the relationship on a fairly cordial note, Joe had come to the conclusion that unless something drastically changed, he was never going to get married.

His expectations were just too high. Worse yet, they were based on a woman who had never really existed. Still, they were stuck in his head, and he couldn't seem to shake them loose. Sweetness and generosity, kindness and good nature, a sense of humor, and a deep, abiding love that would last until they were both old and gray and beyond.

He sighed as he climbed out of the Mustang and headed for the back door into the shop. Syl was back, the woman who had broken his heart, and now that she was here, he realized he still felt the pull of attraction he had felt for her the first time he had seen her that autumn day on the Dreyerville College campus.

The weather was perfect, though the leaves had begun to turn, and in her bright yellow sweater, she was as pretty as the day. He'd asked her out and she had agreed, and they were together nearly every day after that. They were so well matched, like two pieces of a puzzle that fit perfectly together. Whenever he was about to lose patience over a class assignment, she could soothe him with a word or a touch. When she began worrying too much about an upcoming exam, his solid, practical advice often helped melt her fears away. They had been so compatible. Or at least it had seemed that way.

Not that they didn't argue. Syl had a temper and so did he, and both of them felt free to speak their mind.

Which was why it was so hard to understand what had happened, why in the end, everything he had believed about Sylvia Winters had been wrong. She wasn't sweet and generous and loving. She was flighty and artificial. The love she had professed to feel for him was a lie of the very worst sort.

Joe thought of her standing in the aisle at the grocery store and felt a fresh rush of anger. For the first time in the last four years, he wished he had never come back to Dreyerville.

* * *

"Have you seen him yet?" Mary Webster sat next to Syl on the sofa in her apartment. It was hot outside, the air thick and heavy. Both of them were drinking Diet Coke.

"I ran into him at the grocery store last night after work."

Mary sat forward, eyes wide. "Good lord, what happened?"

"He hates me, that's what happened. He was polite, but I could feel the anger pouring out of him in waves."

"You broke his heart, Syl. It's hard to get over something like that." Mary was taller and more slender than Syl, with dark hair and hazel eyes. Until she got married to Denny Webster six years ago and had two kids, Mary had always been shy.

"He blames me for the years he spent in prison—and I don't blame him. If I'd been honest, maybe he never would have wound up in there."

"You thought you were doing him a favor. You were trying to keep him from ruining his life."

Syl let out a bitter laugh. "And look what a

great job I did." She picked up her icy glass but didn't take a sip. "It took me a while—years, in fact—but eventually, I realized not telling Joe the truth was as much of a betrayal as the awful lies I told. The choice I made was exactly the wrong one."

Mary drank a little of her soda. "At the time, we thought you were doing what was right. I think we both believed you were going to die, Syl."

"I know."

"You've been cancer-free for six years. You've come back to where you belong. You've got to tell him, Syl."

She glanced away. "I know. I should have done it years ago but I . . ."

"But you what?"

"I thought he had probably moved on with his life and it was better to let the past just stay in the past."

Mary sighed. "I guess it's always better to deal with something than ignore it." She fiddled with the frost on the side of her glass. "What do you think he'll do when you tell him?"

Syl shook her head. "I have no idea. What I don't think he'll do is forgive me. I think he'll go right on hating me just like he does now."

"But surely if—"

"I lied to him, Mary. I betrayed his trust. I'm probably the reason Joe never got married. He probably believes all women are like me, that a man doesn't dare trust one. If he does, she'll lie to him and break his heart."

Mary set her glass down on the table. "You're both adults now. Whatever happens, you owe it to yourself as much as Joe."

Syl sighed. "I'm still trying to work up my courage."

Mary got up from the sofa, walked over to Sylvia's phone, and picked it up. "Well, there's no time like the present."

"I don't even know his number."

"It's Saturday. Sometimes they keep the shop open till noon. Maybe he's there."

Syl shook her head. "I can't. Not yet. Soon, though. I promise."

"Don't wait too long."

"I've waited eight years, Mary. That's already way too long."

CHAPTER FIVE

◇◇◇◇◇◇◇◇◇◇◇◇◇

Summer was slipping away. Doris had offered to take Teddy to get what he needed for school, but Lottie couldn't remember if they had already gone shopping or not. Her memory was fading every day.

Lottie was frightened.

Terrified.

At least she was when she remembered.

She glanced up from her musings to discover she was standing on the sidewalk in front of

Tremont's Antiques. She was by herself, so Teddy must be working at his afternoon job. She remembered she had wanted to get out of the house and had decided to go for a walk. She didn't remember the trip downtown, but she was sure she could find her way home.

She turned to look in the window and saw the old hand-painted, gingerbread Victorian shelf clock. The clock never failed to remind her of her mother and the years when she was a little girl. No matter what thoughts slipped away from her, the clock always seemed to center her, to carry her back to a warm time in her past and bring her a kind of peace.

She stared at the clock, watched the little brass pendulum swinging back and forth. A horn honked in the street, startling her for a moment, and she turned away from the window.

Lottie frowned. She was standing on Main Street in the middle of the afternoon. She had no idea how she had gotten there or why she might have come.

A little trickle of fear slipped through her. She told herself not to be frightened. She knew the way home.

Making her way to the corner, she turned and

headed in that direction. She wondered if Teddy was home by now, knew that if he was, Doris would keep an eye on him until she got back.

Lottie wondered how much longer she could keep her grandson from figuring out that something was seriously wrong with her.

＊　＊　＊

Doris spotted Lottie making her way up the front porch steps to her house. For the longest time, the older woman just stood there looking confused. Doris realized the door must be locked and Teddy wasn't home yet to unlock the door. She set her paintbrush next to the little ceramic pitcher she was painting, took off her apron, and hurried out the door.

"I can't seem to find my key," Lottie said as Doris walked up.

"Here, give me your purse." Doris dug the key out of a little zippered compartment and handed it to her friend. It broke her heart to see how fast Lottie's condition was deteriorating. And it worried her. Good Lord, what was going to happen to Teddy?

A couple of times, the thought had occurred to

her that she and Floyd might be able to take him, but Floyd was past sixty, hardly the age to become a father, and Doris had never had children. She had no idea what to do with a boy Teddy's age. It wouldn't be fair to any of them.

Lottie went into the house and Doris returned to her painting. With Floyd busy out in his shop for most of the day, the house seemed so quiet. She thought again of Teddy, but shuddered to think of the disruption a boy his age would cause. As much as she wished she could help, she simply wasn't up to it.

She heard the faint buzz of Floyd's saw and remembered when they were first married, how the two of them had worked together down at the cleaners. They had loved each other back then, perhaps not in the way two teenagers would, not with all the passion and turmoil, but they were best friends and they enjoyed each other's company. She wondered what had happened to make it end.

For an instant, she thought of taking him a glass of tea. Floyd liked it with lots of ice and plenty of sugar. It could get pretty hot in the shop, even with the window air conditioner running. But he would be busy sawing and nailing, building his little wooden birdhouses, and he probably wouldn't even notice she was there. She'd end up just setting the glass down and leaving.

With a sigh, she picked up her paintbrush and fixed her attention on the little ceramic pitcher. She had a nice spot for it on one of the shelves over by the window. Of course, Floyd wouldn't notice.

Doris told herself she didn't care.

* * *

It was Saturday afternoon, the end of the first week of September. The time had come. She couldn't put it off any longer.

Today, Syl was going to tell Joe.

Dressed in jeans and a short-sleeved yellow top, she checked her appearance in the mirror, fluffed her tawny hair a little, and added some lipstick. Taking a long, deep breath, she headed for her car. Mary had told her Joe lived in a little house a few blocks away from his shop. In the phone book, he was listed at 225 Jefferson Street. Mary said he usually walked to work, but he probably wouldn't be working on Saturday afternoon.

Syl had considered calling him, trying to set a time, but she was afraid if she phoned, he wouldn't agree to see her. Instead, she was taking the chance she would catch him off guard and he would let her in.

She found the house, which was built in the 1930s or 1940s like most of the houses downtown, and pulled up to the curb in front. The yard had been recently mowed and the shrubs all neatly trimmed. She wasn't sure he would have been so meticulous in his younger days, but then, this was a different Joe from the one she had known.

She walked up beneath the covered porch and rapped lightly on the screen door. She could hear movement inside the house, so she knew someone was home. A few minutes later, Joe pulled open the door and looked out through the screen.

He saw her but he didn't say a word.

"I was hoping you would be here," she said. "I came by to . . . to talk to you."

Through the screen, his blue eyes looked icy cold. "Eight years, and now you want to talk."

"I know you're angry. You have every right to be. But as you said, it's been eight years."

"Yeah, and now you're back."

"I make a mistake, Joe. I did everything wrong, and now I just want it all out in the open."

She could see the tension in his shoulders, knew he was working to hold on to his control. "You made a mistake?" he asked. "That's how you see it? You just made a simple mistake? Lady, you have a helluva lot of nerve coming here. Get off my porch and leave me alone."

He started to close the door in her face.

"Wait! I just . . . give me fifteen minutes, Joe. I just need fifteen minutes. We're both living in Dreyerville. It'll be easier for both of us if you know the truth. Hear me out, and then I'll leave and I won't ever bother you again."

He scoffed. "You want me to know the truth? I don't think you'd recognize the truth if it jumped up and bit you." But he swung open the screen door, and she collected her courage and walked past him into the house.

It was as neat as the yard, a man's house with a dark brown vinyl sofa and chair and inexpensive oak tables. There was a bookcase filled with books against one wall and a small TV on a stand next to a magazine rack. A *Newsweek* sat on top. Joe had always been interested in current events.

"Have a seat," he said, then kind of threw himself into the overstuffed brown vinyl chair.

Syl sat down stiffly, trying not to wither under Joe's murderous regard, knowing she deserved every one of his disdainful glances.

"So what is it you came here to tell me?" he pressed, as if the sooner it was over, the sooner she could be gone.

She took a deep breath and tried to keep her hands from shaking, told herself she could do this. "I lied about everything. Not one word of what I told you was true."

"Big surprise." He stood up, a large man and tall, his stance a little threatening. "Now get out."

Syl held her ground. She was only going to say this once. She didn't have the courage to leave and come back again. "I was sick. That's the reason I left. Two days after we . . . after that night at the lake, I found out I had cervical cancer."

Joe sank slowly back down in his chair.

"They told me I would have to have surgery. Chicago had some of the best doctors for that sort of thing, and my Aunt Bess lived there. Afterward, I had to have chemotherapy. There was a long period of recovery. At the time, I wasn't sure I would . . . survive."

Joe said nothing.

"I didn't . . . didn't want to put you through that, Joe."

"For God's sake, Syl." When he sat forward on the edge of the chair, his usually dark complexion looked a little pale.

"I decided to lie to you, tell you I didn't . . . that I didn't love you. I made everything up. I thought it was better that way."

"Let me get this straight. You said you didn't love me. You lied about that?"

"I was crazy in love with you, Joe. That's why I had to go away."

He seemed to be fighting to make sense of what she was saying. "Are you . . . are you all right now?"

"I've been more than six years cancer free."

Joe's jaw hardened. The anger he felt seemed to eat through his control, and he shot up out of his chair. "Damn you! Damn you, Syl, for what you did! How the hell could you do it? How could you just walk away?"

She started crying. She had promised herself she wouldn't, but this was Joe and she had loved him so much, and when she looked at him, she couldn't seem to help herself. "I'm sorry, Joe. If . . . if I had known what would happen——"

"If you'd known I'd end up in prison, you would have been honest with me? You would have let me help you? Can you really believe it was easier for me to lose you than to be with you when you needed me most?"

She swallowed past the thick lump in her throat. "I thought you would finish college. I thought you would find someone else to love—someone who would live a long life and be there with you when you were both old and gray. I thought you would find someone who could give you children. I knew how much you wanted a family."

"We both wanted children. We were going to have a houseful of kids—that's what we said."

"I'm . . . I'm sterile, Joe."

His throat moved up and down. For a moment, he looked away. On a shaky breath, he turned back to her. "All those years . . . all those years I hated you. Now I look at you and I feel . . . dammit, Syl, I don't know what I feel."

"I never meant to hurt you the way I did."

"What about you, Syl? Did you hurt, too, or was it just me?"

"I thought I was dying. When I lost you, I did

die a little. I died inside, Joe. It took me years to make a life for myself."

"But you did, and now you've come back. I wish you'd stayed in Chicago."

Fresh tears welled. "At least you know the truth. Maybe that's one of the reasons I came home. I owed you the truth. I have since the day I left."

His eyes narrowed. "It doesn't really change anything. You lied to me. You betrayed my trust."

"I know. At least now, maybe you can start to forgive me."

A muscle tightened in his jaw.

Syl stood up on wobbly legs and started for the door. She heard Joe's deep voice behind her.

"Imagine where we'd be now, Syl, if you'd told me the truth back then."

She turned to face him. "It was a hard time, Joe. Who knows where we would be."

"*I* know," he said firmly. "I think you do, too."

Syl said nothing more. Her lies had destroyed whatever there had once been between them.

There was only mistrust and sadness now. She held back a sob as she hurried out the door.

✳ ✳ ✳

Joe watched Syl step out onto the porch, and then he closed the door behind her.

All those years, all the rage he had felt, the betrayal. He'd gotten into a fistfight because some guy down at the bar had said how hot Syl was and asked if Joe had gotten into her pants.

Just the mention of her name had infuriated him, and yet he had found himself defending her, throwing a roundhouse punch that had wound up killing a man. Three years in prison had cooled his temper, but not the rage he felt inside. Not his fury.

All because the woman he loved hadn't loved him enough to trust him. Instead of accepting his help and support, she had suffered through cancer on her own. She had lied to protect him. Or so she believed. Instead, she had nearly destroyed him. He felt sick to his stomach.

Walking into the kitchen, he turned on the tap, poured himself a glass of water, and then downed it a single, long gulp. His hands were shaking. He wiped the perspiration off his forehead with the sleeve of his shirt.

She had come back to Dreyerville to tell him the truth.

As he had said, he wished she hadn't come.

It was easier to hang on to his hatred, easier to believe she was nothing at all like the woman he had meant to make his wife. Now, his stomach churned to think of what she had suffered, of all they had lost. And there was this thing going on inside him, feelings for her he couldn't quite make go away. For an instant, when he had seen her on the porch, it wasn't rage he'd felt but a deep, long-buried yearning.

It didn't matter.

Perhaps another man could set the past aside and consider they might still have a future. After the damage she had done and the years he had lost, Joe just wasn't that man.

※　※　※

Sylvia stood at her desk in Dr. Davis's office. She had always wanted to be a nurse, and she was a good one. Which was why, for the last six months, she had been thinking of taking the classes necessary to become a physician's assistant. It would take two long years, but she had plenty of spare time and she looked forward to the challenge. Two weeks ago, she had registered for night classes at Dreyerville Community College and had started school last night.

With her job and the night classes and seeing

old friends, her life should have been full, and yet as each day passed, Syl felt as if something were missing. Maybe it was seeing Joe again, remembering the life they had planned to share, thinking of all she had lost when she had left him.

Maybe it was the way she still felt whenever she thought of him.

Whatever it was, in time, it would pass. She had survived the terrible ordeal of cancer. She could survive a few bittersweet memories.

She looked down at the appointment book lying on top of the desk.

"Who's Dr. Davis got next?" she asked the young blond receptionist.

The girl looked down at the name written next to the one-thirty spot. "Mrs. Sparks."

Just then, Syl heard the buzzer over the door as it opened, and Doris Culver walked in, followed by Lottie Sparks. Syl took in the older woman's slightly stooped posture, the silver hair that was a bit less neatly combed. Each week, the woman looked a little paler, a little more fragile, her eyes a little more distant. There was no cure for Alzheimer's, but there were some new drugs being tested that seemed to slow the process a bit. They were called acetylcholinesterase inhibitors. Dr. Davis was considering their use in Lottie Sparks's case, but he wasn't sure how much good the drugs would actually do.

Lottie walked up to the desk. "Good morning . . ."—she read Syl's badge—"Sylvia." Like many Alzheimer's patients, Lottie was becoming a master of hiding her memory problems. She would wait for clues, something that might help her remember, or simply leave out the mention of a name and keep the conversation friendly but impersonal.

Syl smiled a greeting at Doris, who stood a few feet away, then returned her attention to the patient. "It's nice to see you, Lottie. Dr. Davis is ready for you." *Both of you,* Syl mentally corrected. The disease had progressed to the point where Lottie needed someone with her during the appointment. Doris had become that someone.

"If you'll both just follow me . . ."

Lottie frowned, obviously confused.

"It's all right, dear," Doris said gently. "You've got an appointment with Dr. Davis, remember?"

Lottie smiled and nodded. "Oh, that's right, Dr. Davis," she said, but Syl wasn't sure she actually recalled.

Lottie and Doris followed her down the hall into

one of the examining rooms. Syl left them, and a few minutes later, Dr. Davis joined them in the room.

It was a brief appointment, mostly just a physical checkup. The women reappeared not long after and made their way out of the office. Sylvia thought of Lottie's grandson and wondered how much longer Teddy would be able to stay in the house with her. She wondered if he might have some family somewhere who would volunteer to take care of him, but from what Doris had said, she didn't think so.

She wondered if he would wind up in the foster care system and what would become of him once they took him away.

＊　＊　＊

Joe watched young Teddy Sparks push the heavy broom across the floor of the repair shop waiting room. The kid was a damned hard worker. He never complained, never once shirked a job, no matter how dirty it was. Lately, Joe had started to bring him into the shop, let him watch while he changed a tire or replaced a battery, showed him how to use the grease gun, which seemed to thrill him no end.

Everything in the shop seemed to interest Teddy. Either engines were in a guy's blood, or they weren't, and Joe was betting they were in Teddy's. No doubt the kid was already dreaming about the hot car he was going to buy when he was old enough to drive.

"I want a car like your Mustang, Joe," Teddy said. "It's really great."

Joe just laughed. He remembered working with his dad in the garage behind their house, remembered how just the smell of grease and rubber made him smile. His dad was dead now, a heart attack at the age of fifty. His mom lived in a condo in L.A., something he never would have imagined. But Joe liked small-town living, liked owning his own business, liked how good he was at fixing cars.

It was fun to share a little of his knowledge with Teddy, a boy who seemed to enjoy it as much as Joe did. Last week, Teddy had started third grade, but Joe had offered to let him keep working a couple of hours after school.

The boy was here today, working hard as always, but Joe had noticed the slight frown tucked between his usually warm brown eyes. Joe walked over and caught the handle of the broom.

"Nice job. You're getting real good at this sweeping stuff."

Teddy grinned. "Does that mean I can use the grease gun again?"

"I think maybe it can be arranged." Joe leaned the broom against the wall. "You look like you were thinking pretty hard on something. You want to tell me what it is?"

Teddy's smile slid away. "I was thinking about my gramma."

"Yeah? What about her?"

"She keeps forgetting things. Last night, she left the burner on under a pot on the stove. The whole kitchen filled up with smoke."

Joe was afraid that sooner or later, something like that might happen. He had noticed the older woman's forgetfulness, which seemed to be escalating with every visit.

"You talk to her about it?"

Teddy shook his head, moving thick dark strands of hair around his ears. "I didn't wanna hurt her feelings." He looked up, his features bright once more. "The clock she likes is still in the window at Tremont's. I almost got enough saved to put a down payment on it."

Joe smiled. "That's great, Teddy." He knew how much the boy wanted to buy the clock. Last week, Joe had talked to Mr. Tremont and asked him to hold the clock until Teddy could make the down payment. He'd told the man he would personally guarantee the purchase.

"I can't wait to see Gramma's face when I give it to her at Christmas."

"I'm sure she'll love it. It'll mean a lot that you saved your money to buy it for her."

A noise intruded, and Teddy's gaze swung to the door. Joe turned and spotted a dark-haired woman standing in the opening.

"May I help you?" he asked, walking toward her.

"You're Joe Dixon, the owner of the shop?"

"Half owner, yes."

"I'm Emma Kingsley. I'm raising money for the Dreyerville Women's Shelter. The ladies who run the program suggested I stop by. They said they can always count on you for a donation."

Joe smiled. "The shelter does important work. I'll be happy to donate. While I write a check, why don't you put one of those collection jars up on the counter? I'll see if I can stir up a little more money from my customers."

The woman's eyes brightened. "Why, thank you so much, Mr. Dixon."

Teddy helped Mrs. Kingsley set up the display, and Joe returned with a check.

"Your son is a darling boy."

"Teddy's a good kid," Joe said, not bothering to correct her. He handed her the donation, wishing he could afford to give more. But he was sure he could get his customers to come up with a little extra for the pot.

He and Teddy went back to work putting things in order in the shop. As he watched Teddy work, it occurred to him that if he and Syl had gotten married, if their lives had gone the way they had planned, they might have had a son almost Teddy's age.

But Syl had gotten sick, and even if she had told him the truth about her illness and they had stayed together, there would have been no children.

At the end of the day, as Teddy climbed onto his bicycle and rode off toward his house, Joe realized how much he wished things could have been different.

CHAPTER SIX

◇◇◇◇◇◇◇◇◇◇◇◇◇◇◇◇◇

September crept into October. The huge, sprawling sycamore next to Syl's above-garage apartment turned a brilliant orange-red and began to lose its leaves. The rolling hillsides bloomed with autumn colors. Russet and gold wreathed the lake at the south end of town.

Unable to resist the lure of the crisp fall weather and changing seasons, Syl packed herself a picnic lunch and drove out to the lake on a Saturday afternoon. There was only one other vehicle parked in the narrow dirt lot. She could barely see it through the trees. Syl parked a ways away, took her lunch and her Kodak camera, and headed for one of the tables down by the water.

An old wooden dock, slightly tilted to one side but sturdy enough to be used by amateur fishermen, pushed its way out into the lake. Two figures stood on the dock, she saw, a boy and a man, both of them dark-haired.

"Miss Winters!" the boy called out, waving madly. It was Teddy Sparks, she realized, as he handed his pole to the man and raced toward her down the dock.

Her stomach contracted when Joe Dixon stood up from where he'd crouched next to Teddy. She hadn't seen him since that day at his house, and she didn't want to see him now.

Teddy slid to a stop in front of her. His arrival steadied her nerves and put an end to the rolling in her stomach.

"Miss Winters! You gotta come! You gotta see what we caught!" He reached out and caught her hand. Syl couldn't help smiling at his excitement. And she couldn't refuse to go with him, even if seeing Joe was the last thing she wanted.

"Hurry up!" He tugged her forward. Her camera dangled from her wrist, along with the bag that held her lunch: a turkey sandwich, an apple, a bag of Fritos, and a Snickers bar for dessert.

The dock moved under her feet as Teddy led her forward, stopping right next to Joe.

"Me and Joe—we caught four fish! Look how big this one is." Teddy proudly held up one of the fish, which was at least eighteen inches long. "Joe says he's gonna fry him for dinner."

Syl looked up at Joe.

The fake smile he mustered lifted the edges of his mouth. "You always did like to come out to the lake."

Syl flushed. They used to park at the lake as often as they could. This wasn't the same lake where they had made love, but the reference was clear. Syl had never forgotten that night. Apparently, Joe hadn't, either.

For Teddy's sake, she managed a smile. "It was such a nice day, I thought I would treat myself to a picnic."

Teddy grinned. "We were just gonna eat our lunch, weren't we, Joe? Why don't you come and eat with us?"

Joe's face was a thundercloud. She racked her

brain for some excuse not to join them, but her mind refused to come up with anything remotely believable.

Teddy dropped the fish into a woven creel sitting at Joe's feet. "Come on, Joe, I'm hungry. I bet Miss Winters is, too."

She had been hungry when she arrived at the lake. Now she couldn't imagine swallowing a single bite of food.

Joe picked up the creel and slung it over his shoulder. He'd always had wide shoulders, and if anything, they were even more muscular now. He grabbed a pole and handed it to Teddy and picked up his own, and the three of them started back down the dock.

There were tables along the edge of the water. One of them had a red-checked plastic cloth draped over it and a brown paper bag sitting on top.

"Joe made roast beef sandwiches," Teddy said. "They're my favorite."

Still scowling, Joe reached into the bag and started setting paper plates out on the table. He set one down in front of her, along with a paper napkin for each of them. A cooler rested at the far end of the table.

"We've got Coke," Joe said. "I know you women usually drink Diet."

"Regular's fine. It's a picnic. I get to splurge."

Joe put out the food, Syl put out the lunch she had brought, and they sat down on benches across from each other. As Teddy kept up a running conversation, eventually the tension in Joe's face began to ease. Teddy smiled up at him, and Joe smiled back. He had always liked children. It was clear he had come to care a great deal for Teddy.

"Can I fish some more?" the boy asked, the first one to clean up his plate.

"Don't go out on the dock. You can fish off the bank at the edge of the water. Just be sure to stay where I can see you."

Teddy looked wistfully at the dock where they had caught the big fish, but didn't complain. He was such a sweet boy. Maybe Joe would be willing to take him, if it came to that. The thought abruptly faded. Joe was a convicted felon. There was no way they would let him have the boy.

"So how's work going?" he asked, which returned her attention to Joe. She could feel his gaze on her and ignored a thread of longing.

"I got lucky. I've always liked nursing, and

Dr. Davis's office is a really good place to work. I'm also taking night classes to get my requirements to become a physician's assistant."

"Good for you."

"What about you? Mary says you're buying Mr. Murdock's interest in his auto repair shop."

He nodded. "Bumper wants to retire. I own half the place already. At night, I'm taking business classes at the college. I plan to open repair shops all over the state."

"You'll do it. You always did what you set out to."

His smile turned feral. "You're taking night classes and so am I. Maybe we'll run into each other at school. It'll be just like the old days."

The words knifed into her heart. "Joe . . . I know . . . after what I did . . . we're never going to be friends, but—"

"You're right, Syl." He straightened on the bench, a move that made him look even taller than he usually did. "The last thing I want is to be your friend." His eyes ran over her in a way they never had before, and a little curl of heat slid into her stomach. "I could never be friends with a woman I'd still like to have in my bed."

Syl just sat there. Joe had never spoken to her that way, not even when they were engaged to be married. Clearly, he had done it to shock her, to punish her in some way for the pain she had caused him. Instead, when he had assessed her with that hot look in his eyes and a jaw turned to steel, she had never felt so womanly, so seductive. And she had never felt the fierce heat that was burning through her now.

But Joe was no longer the boy he had been back then. At twenty-nine, he was a full-grown male.

With stunning clarity and panic in her heart, Syl realized she was far more attracted to the man he had become than she had ever been to the boy he was before.

✳ ✳ ✳

Standing at the edge of the lake next to Teddy, Joe watched Syl's little Honda Civic pull out of the parking lot. She had made an excuse to leave just minutes after he had made his off-color remark.

He shouldn't have said what he did. He had never spoken to a woman that way before. But every time he saw her, the past seemed to surface, to rise up with agonizing force. Memories of lazy fall days on campus, the two of them lying beneath an ancient sycamore, Syl's head in his lap as she studied for a test. Thoughts of shared afternoons by the pond.

He remembered the winter they had gone sledding. The snow had been soft and deep, the sun so bright it hurt his eyes. He had pushed the sled off a rise and jumped in behind her. The sled had flown as if it had wings until it hit a rock beneath the snow. He remembered how they had flown into the air and Syl had landed on top of him. He remembered their laughter, the soft kiss that made him want more.

He thought of the brutal days after she had left, the drinking and fighting, the trial and the days he had spent in prison. He thought of the hard, ruthless man he'd become just to survive inside those thick, gray walls.

It had taken him years to recover, to make a life for himself, to find his rightful place in the world. Then Syl had come back and his peaceful existence threatened to crumble, just as it had before.

Every time he saw her, a haze of anger settled over him. He wanted to make her pay for all the suffering she had caused.

He wanted to erase all the pain she had endured, the fear and the heartbreak.

He wanted to turn back time, wanted to be there when she needed him.

Today, he had discovered, he just plain wanted her.

Joe sighed as he stared out over the water. No other woman had ever stirred him the way Syl could with a simple smile. No other woman had ever heated his blood with a single glance. He thought he was over her, had told himself so a thousand times.

Now he realized he would never be over Sylvia Winters.

And the question became, what the hell was he going to do about it?

※　※　※

Rainy weather set in. Dense gray, flat-bottomed clouds loomed overhead, and the temperature began to drop. Doris put the final touches on the little Pinocchio statue she was painting, coloring his floppy hat a rich, deep blue that matched his shoes, and then she set the figurine down to dry on the kitchen table.

Through the walls of the kitchen, she could hear the faint buzz of Floyd's saw cutting small round holes in the wooden birdhouses he sold over at the mercantile. On impulse, Doris grabbed a mug and reached for the gently boiling teapot on the stove. She dropped a bag of Earl Grey into the mug, added a heaping teaspoon of sugar, just the way Floyd liked, and dunked the bag a couple of times. A second impulse had her setting the mug down on the counter long enough to untie the apron from around the waist of her jeans and pull up the sleeves of her sweater. Then she grabbed the mug and sailed out the door.

When she reached the garage, she paused, though she wasn't quite sure why. Just to catch her breath, she told herself, using the moment to smooth an errant strand of pale hair back into the neat chignon at the nape of her neck.

Inside the shop, she spotted Floyd where he stood behind the jigsaw, an average man, bald and a little overweight. Doris smiled and held up the steaming mug in answer to the unspoken question in his eyes.

"It's so cold and blustery," she said. "I thought this might warm you a bit."

Floyd looked surprised and a little uncertain. She rarely invaded his domain, and she couldn't remember the last time she had done so simply to bring him a cup of tea.

"You didn't wreck the car, did you?"

Her bright smile wobbled. She shouldn't have come. "Don't be silly. I just thought you might like something warm to drink."

Floyd took the mug, bent his head over the cup, and inhaled the brisk aroma. "Smells good." He took a small sip and looked up. "You sure nothing's wrong?"

She managed to keep her smile in place. "Not a thing. Like I said, I just . . . I thought you might like some tea."

He grunted a reply and took a drink, and a sort of calm seemed to wash over him. "Thanks."

Turning away from her, he took another sip, set the mug down next to the saw, and went back to work. For several long moments, Doris stood there watching him, a soft yearning in her chest.

Then she turned and walked back to the house, wondering what had possessed her to come out to the shop in the first place.

CHAPTER SEVEN

Syl sat at Doris's kitchen table sipping jasmine tea. They both liked it sweet and hot, especially on a cold, rainy day like this one, though Syl took hers with a little milk or cream.

Doris blew across her mug, cooling it a bit. On Saturdays, she only worked till noon and it was well past that now. "Teddy came over for a visit yesterday. He likes to watch Floyd work. I told Floyd he had to be careful with the saw whenever the boy was around."

"Teddy seems to be interested in anything he can build or repair," said Syl. "He's smart and he's incredibly sweet. I worry what will happen to him."

"So do I." Doris took a sip from her mug, but over the rim, her eyes remained on Syl's face. "Teddy mentioned his fishing trip last weekend. He said he had a picnic with you and Joe out at the lake."

Syl's shoulders tightened. "It wasn't a date or anything. I drove out to take some pictures. The fall colors were just so pretty, I couldn't resist. When I got there, Joe was there with Teddy."

"So how'd it go?"

"How did what go?"

"I might be getting old, but I'm not that old. I saw the way you looked at him that day at the supermarket. I saw the way he looked at you. You could feel the sizzle in the air from at least ten feet away." Syl had finally told Doris the truth, that she had broken her engagement to Joe because she had been fighting cancer.

"I think we both feel some of the old attraction. I'm sure it's just physical. We were in love once. Maybe both of us fantasize a little about what it might have been like if we had stayed together."

"If you're attracted to each other, why don't you do something about it? Joe's not married. Neither are you. What's to keep you from exploring where that attraction might lead?"

Syl shook her head. "Too many hard feelings. I don't think Joe will ever be able to forgive me for the years he spent in prison. It was my fault and—"

"Hold it right there, missy. What happened to Joe Dixon was caused by Joe Dixon. Sure, your leaving left him an angry man, but it wasn't you who threw the punch that wound up killing a man."

"No, but still . . ."

"Joe isn't a fool. He might like to blame you for what happened. It's a lot easier that way, but deep down, he knows the truth. In time, he'll come to grips with the way things were then and the way they are now. You just need to nudge him along in the right direction."

A sad smile rose on Syl's lips. "I can't do that, Doris. Even if you were right and we started dating, it might not work out. If it didn't, I couldn't survive losing Joe again. I'm just not willing to take the risk."

Doris was about to start arguing when flashing red lights lit up the kitchen walls. Since not much happened in the sleepy little town of Dreyerville, both women set their mugs down and raced over to the window.

A police car rolled up to the curb in front of Lottie Sparks's house. There were two policemen inside the vehicle. One got out and opened the rear passenger door to let someone out, while the other started toward Doris's house.

"Oh, good Lord," Doris said. "Something must have happened to Lottie." She ran out of the kitchen, and Syl followed. When they stepped out on the porch, the officer who had been driving was climbing the front porch steps.

"Are you Mrs. Culver?" He was young, blond, and good-looking. He didn't seem old enough to be a policeman, though it was clear he was.

"Why, yes, I am. Is Lottie all right? Mrs. Sparks . . . is she all right?"

"She's had some trouble." He flicked a glance at the house next door, where the other patrolman, tall and rangy with light brown hair, escorted Lottie inside. "It seems she drove her car down to the post office then couldn't find her way back home. She parked the car and walked back to the post office to ask for help, and they called us."

"How did you know where she lived?" Doris asked.

"Driver's license."

"Oh . . . yes, of course."

"She said we should speak to you. Apparently, the two of you are friends."

"That's right. I've known Lottie Sparks for more than twenty years."

"Will you be able to pick up her car? She's not going to be able to drive anymore."

"I can take you down to get it," Syl offered. "Then you can drive it back to the house."

"She's parked at the corner of Elm and Fifth," the policeman told Doris, "and you'll need to keep her keys."

"I understand." Doris accepted the car keys the officer handed her. "She hardly ever drives anymore. The post office isn't that far away. She usually walks, but it's been raining off and on. I guess that's why she drove there today."

"Alzheimer's patients often forget what they should or shouldn't be doing," Syl added softly.

"I had a hunch that was the situation here," said young Officer Collins, the name on his badge. "We see this kind of thing fairly often with elderly people. I hope she doesn't live alone."

"She . . . um . . . lives with her grandson." Syl didn't add that the boy was only eight years old. She would speak to Dr. Davis, see what should be done, and keep an eye on Teddy until they could figure things out. Considering what had happened today, it was clear Lottie couldn't take care of Teddy any longer.

"Is the boy underage?" the officer asked, the question falling like a blow.

Syl looked over at Doris.

"I'm afraid so," Doris said.

The officer took a notepad out of his shirt pocket and scribbled down a note. "I'll have to inform Social Services, report what happened. Odds are, the boy won't be able to stay with her from now on. Does he have any other family, someone who might be willing to take him in?"

"Not as far as I know." Doris glanced over her shoulder, toward the workshop behind the house. "I—I could take him for a while . . . until you can find him a home."

The officer jotted another note. "As much as I wish I could let you, that isn't possible . . . at least not right now. There are certain procedures we have to follow. I hope you understand. If you're interested, you can go down and file an application." He glanced toward the door. "Where is the boy now?"

"He's probably at work," Syl answered. "He works part-time for Joe Dixon, down at Murdock's Auto Repair."

The policeman nodded. "We'll pick him up and tell him what's happened. They'll keep him at the county facility until they can check things out."

Syl felt a wave of pity. Dear God, poor little Teddy. He had no father. He had lost his mother. Now he was losing his grandmother, the only family he had left. It was too much for one little boy.

"Like I said, you can go down and talk to them if you're serious about taking him, but the placement would have to be permanent. That's the way it works."

Doris made no reply. Syl had a feeling she wasn't up to taking on that kind of responsibility. Neither of the Culvers was prepared to raise a child Teddy's age. It wouldn't be fair to the Culvers, or to Teddy.

Doris's head jerked up from her musings. "Ohmygosh, wait a minute! About six months ago, Lottie gave me a letter. She said I should open it if something happened to her. I think maybe she meant this kind of thing. I'll go get it." Doris dashed back inside the house.

The screen door slammed behind her as a bright red Mustang splashed through the mud puddles at the curb and braked to a stop behind the patrol car next door. Joe Dixon sat behind the wheel, Teddy in the passenger seat. Joe turned off the engine, and both of them climbed out. Even from a distance, Syl could see Joe staring at the patrol car and frowning. She forced herself to call out to him from the porch.

"Joe! Could you and Teddy come over here for a minute?"

Joe urged Teddy toward Doris's house, and they started up the wooden steps. Joe cast Syl an unreadable glance, then turned his attention to the patrolman.

"What's going on here, Officer?"

The young cop recapped the events of the day, filling Joe in, then turning to Teddy, careful to make sure the boy understood what was happening with his grandmother, that her memory was failing and what that meant to him.

"I'm sorry, son. You won't be able to stay with your grandma." He smiled, trying to soften the blow. "At least not right now."

Fear flashed in Teddy's eyes. "I know she forgets things sometimes, but I can take care of her. If I'd been with her today, she would'n'a got lost."

The policeman looked up at Joe. "I take it he works for you."

"I'm his friend, Joe Dixon. Teddy does odd jobs for me over at Murdock's Auto. Nothing official, he's just earning some money for Christmas. I'm not breaking any child labor laws or anything."

"That's not a problem."

"Teddy usually rides his bicycle to and from the garage, but it was raining pretty hard, so I drove him home."

"It's clear you're concerned, but there's not much you can do to help Teddy today. There are laws, rules to be followed. They're put in place for the benefit and safety of the child. I'm afraid Teddy will have to come with me."

"What will happen to him?" Joe asked.

"We'll try to find a family member who'll take him. If not, Social Services will have to find a placement for him."

"I want to stay with my gramma," Teddy said, panic in his face.

The policeman crouched beside him. "You can't stay here, son. Your grandma just can't handle it anymore."

Syl could see the tension in Joe's broad

shoulders. "I don't suppose you would let him stay with me."

The officer shook his head. "Mrs. Culver offered, as well. If we just turned him over to someone without any sort of investigation, we could be guilty of child endangerment."

Teddy reached up and took hold of Joe's hand. "Joe, I'm scared."

Joe lowered himself to Teddy's level and looked into his eyes. "We'll work this out, son, I promise. I'll do whatever it takes to find a good place for you to live, a place where you'll be happy."

"Why can't I stay with you?"

"I wish you could, Teddy. Maybe we can find a way. . . ."

But Syl could tell by the tight constriction of his throat that Joe didn't believe it was possible. Not with his criminal record.

"Time to go, son," the officer said, reaching a hand out to Teddy.

When Teddy didn't take it, Joe scooped him up in his arms and carried him off down the steps toward the patrol car. The second officer was waiting. He opened the rear door, and Joe settled the boy in the backseat. Syl couldn't hear what Joe was saying, but she could tell that Teddy was crying.

The young blond policeman was about to leave the porch when Doris came barreling out the screen door.

"Here's the letter," Doris said, tearing open the envelope as she reached them, beginning to scan the words.

"What's it say?" Syl asked.

Doris took a breath and started to read.

Dear Doris,

If you are reading this, something must have happened. I knew it would, sooner or later. I just pray that by now my Teddy has a loving home. If he doesn't, I beg you as a friend who has become very dear to me that you will help him find one. I want you to know that my Chester left me in very solid financial shape, so there are funds enough for whatever needs to be done to take care of me and also money for Teddy's college education.

Doris stopped reading. Digging a Kleenex out of the pocket of her jeans, she wiped the tears from her cheek and handed the letter to Syl with a shaking hand. "You finish it," she said, her voice thick with emotion.

Syl swallowed past the lump in her throat.

> *Tell Teddy how much I love him. Tell him he is the light of my life and always will be. Tell him to remember me, but please don't burden him with my illness. Thank you for being such a dear, dear friend.*
>
> *Lottie.*

Syl looked up, her own eyes moist with tears. "The name of her bank and the account numbers are written at the bottom of the page. I think she meant for you to manage the money. I imagine she must have made some sort of arrangement with the bank."

Doris took the letter and reread the words. "We'll get her in-home care," she said, "someone who'll be good to her. It sounds like she'll be able to afford it."

"That's a good idea. I'm sure she'd rather stay in her own home."

The officer spoke up just then. Syl had almost forgotten he was there.

"We've got your name and address, Mrs. Culver. Give me your phone number, and I'll keep you posted on the boy."

Doris did as he asked and then the policeman was gone.

The last thing Syl saw was little Teddy's face pressed again the window of the patrol car as he waved good-bye to Joe.

✳ ✳ ✳

It was not a good week for anyone. Teddy was staying at the county facility for orphans and children who were victims of abuse. Doris had hired a woman named Phyllis Williams to live at the Sparks's house and take care of Lottie, but Lottie wasn't dealing with her new companion well.

"I don't need anyone to take care of me," she grumbled on a daily basis. "I can take care of myself!"

Doris spent hours talking to her, reminding her about the Alzheimer's and what was happening to her, repeating the same information again and again.

By the end of that first week, something must have clicked, at least for a while, because the complaining had mostly stopped. Lottie had asked about Teddy at least a thousand times and been told he was doing just fine. No one had the courage to tell her he was living in a county facility, soon to be placed in a foster home, even though Lottie wouldn't have remembered.

According to Doris, Joe had gone down to see Teddy every day since the boy had been taken from Lottie's home. He had filed an application to become Teddy's foster parent, but with his criminal record, he held little hope. Syl was surprised when she spotted Joe's Mustang pulling up in front of the house. Her nerves kicked in even more when a few minutes later, she heard him climb the stairs and knock at her door.

With a steadying breath, she walked over and pulled it open. "Hello, Joe."

"Hi . . ." He stepped into the living room, though she hadn't thought to invite him in.

"I . . . uh . . . know I should have called, but every time I thought about it, I lost my nerve."

"That's all right. I just got home from church. I didn't have anything planned."

"Presbyterian, right? I saw you there with Doris."

"You were there this morning? You go to church?"

He shrugged those wide, quarterback shoulders. "I started after I got out of prison. I don't go all the time. I sort of deal with God in my own way, but still . . . it's nice once in a while. Lately, I figured I could use the help."

"With Teddy, you mean."

"Yeah."

"I didn't see you there."

"I was standing at the back. I can slip out easier that way."

He walked farther into the living room, took a look at the plants she had placed on tables in front of the windows, the flowered, fringed throws she had tossed over the old sofa and chairs, the watercolors she had bought at a flea market in Chicago, had framed, and hung on the walls.

"I knew you'd be good at this kind of thing . . . decorating a place, making it feel like home."

"You think so?"

"Yeah." He looked over at a photo of the lake she had taken last winter in Chicago. "Nice picture. You take it?"

She nodded. "I was just going over the ones I took out at the lake. The colors were so pretty that day. . . . I thought I might have a couple of them blown up and framed." She glanced down, a little embarrassed. "It's kind of a hobby of mine."

Joe started walking toward the table, where she had set the photos out to study them and Syl panicked. He would find the photos she had taken of him! Dear Lord, what would he think?

"Some of these are really nice," he said.

"Thanks." She hurriedly reached out to scoop them up, but it was already too late.

Joe held up a photo of him and Teddy. "I didn't know you took this. Any chance I could get a copy?"

"Sure." She reached for them again, but before she could reach them, he plucked up the one she had taken of him. It was a photo of Joe in profile, his incredible blue eyes and solid jaw, his mouth slightly curved in a smile as he looked down at Teddy, his black hair ruffled by the wind. Joe studied it as if he couldn't quite believe his eyes.

He held up the photo. "Why, Syl?"

She shrugged, though she hardly felt nonchalant. "I like taking pictures. You make a good subject."

"That's all?"

"I like looking at you. I always have."

His eyes ran over her in that hot way that made her feel so sexy. "I like looking at you, too." He took her hand. "Mind if we sit down?"

"No, of course not. I'm just . . . I'm not thinking very clearly. I was . . . you know . . . surprised to
see you here."

"I'm surprised to be here. Well, not exactly surprised. I've been thinking about coming over for a
while. I thought maybe we could talk a little more,
see if we can find a way to get past the hurt and
pain, get beyond the past somehow."

As she stared into his handsome face, an ache
rose up inside her. "Do you think we ever really
could?"

"Maybe. A lot has happened in both of our
lives. Still, when I see you . . . I can't stop thinking
of you, Syl."

Her throat closed up. "I think of you, too, Joe."
He led her over to the sofa, and both of them sat
down. She tried not to think how good it was to
have him sitting there beside her. "How's Teddy?"
she asked.

Joe shook his head. "He's not taking this very
well. They've got some kind of child psychiatrist talking to him. At the end of the week, they're placing him
in what they call an emergency home. He'll be there
until they can find him a permanent placement."

"I feel so sorry for him. I stopped by to see him
a couple of times. He's so completely alone."

"What he needs is someone who will love him." Joe raked a hand through his wavy black hair. "I've put in an application to become his foster parent, but I don't think there's a snowball's chance in hell they'll let me have him. They do a full FBI investigation of anyone who's interested in providing him a home."

"I'm sorry, Joe. I know how much you like kids. I could tell how much you cared for Teddy."

"The system's so screwed up. They'd rather give Teddy to people more interested in the money they'll get for raising him than to someone who would love him and give him a really good home."

"That doesn't always happen."

He sighed. "No, I guess not." He looked so tense, so worried. And weary. Bone weary. For the first time, Syl realized how much Joe had come to love the little boy.

"You want some coffee or something?"

"I'm fine." He caught her hand a second time. His fingers were calloused, yet his touch was gentle. "I'd rather you just sat here and kept me company. Once, you were my best friend in the world. I could use a friend right now."

Something soft swelled inside her. It was followed by a tremor of uncertainty. Surely he wasn't thinking they could pick up where they had left off. "Joe . . ."

"Take it easy. I'm not trying to push you into anything. We don't even know each other anymore."

She relaxed a little. "No, we don't."

"So, how about I take you out to dinner tonight and we make a stab at understanding the people we've become?"

She bit her lip, told herself to say no. She couldn't risk those kinds of feelings again, couldn't survive the pain if it didn't work out. Instead, she found herself nodding, saying, "Okay. What time?"

"I'm going by to see Teddy after work. I'll come get you after that . . . say about six-thirty?"

"Six-thirty sounds great."

But as she watched him rise from the sofa, a sense of panic pressed down on her chest. What he'd said was true. They didn't really know each other anymore. Maybe Joe wanted some sort of revenge for the betrayal she had dealt him and the years he had lost. Maybe he would make her fall in love with him again and then leave her.

The panic expanded into fear, tightening as he walked to the door. Then he turned and smiled down at her in that soft way he used to but hadn't since her return.

"I'll see you tonight," he said.

And Syl was more afraid than she had ever been before.

CHAPTER EIGHT

<hr />

*O*ctober ended cold, and November rushed in with a vengeance. Floyd stood warming his hands over the old pot-bellied stove in his workshop. The wind was blowing outside like ol' Billie hell, and the squat iron stove couldn't seem to throw off enough heat. He could use a hot cup of tea, he thought, and couldn't shake the image of Doris looking so pretty, bringing a steaming mug out to him.

Funny . . . that afternoon had popped into his

head a dozen times, and he couldn't quite figure out why.

"Mr. Culver?"

It was little Teddy Sparks. Poor kid was staying in some kind of temporary foster home until they could find him a permanent placement. Joe Dixon had made an application, Sylvia had said, but with his record, everyone put the odds against him. Too bad, that. Joe had turned his life around, become an upstanding citizen and an asset to the community. And it was clear he loved the boy.

"Come on in, Teddy."

A couple of times a week, Teddy's foster mother dropped him off to spend a couple of hours with his grandmother. The visitation had been ordered by the court, since there was a lady at Lottie's now to watch out for both of them, but Floyd wasn't sure how long it was going to last.

Lottie's memory was failing fast now, and Floyd wondered if she actually even recognized the boy. Teddy usually only stayed an hour or so, then came over to see Floyd in the shop before his foster mother, a sour old gal named Elmira Mack who seemed older than she really was, picked him up.

"Hey, slugger, how you doin'?"

"Doin' okay. Gramma's not so good, though. She doesn't like having that lady in her house." He smiled. "She's always glad to see me, though."

"I'll bet she is."

"The lady, Mrs. Williams, she made us some chocolate-chip cookies, and we ate 'em with a glass of milk."

"That's good, Teddy." Floyd figured maybe Lottie was just glad for the company, even if she wasn't sure who the boy was.

Floyd turned back to the birdhouse he was sanding, and Teddy walked over to watch. "I wanna buy one of those for Miss Winters. I want to give it to her for Christmas."

"I thought you were saving your money to buy that clock for your grandma."

"I already got enough for that. Joe said he'd go down and pick it up for me, keep it for me till Christmas."

Floyd smiled, liking the boy, thinking maybe he and Doris ought to take him. But damned, even if they passed muster, he was just too old to raise an eight-year-old kid. "So, which birdhouse you want?"

There was a shelf of them ready for delivery to the merc. Each one was different, with a separate personality, or so it seemed to Floyd, which was why he enjoyed making them so much.

Teddy looked each one over with the scrutiny of a real horse trader. "I'll take that one up there." He pointed to the third house over.

"This one here?" Floyd set the birdhouse down on the table, and Teddy examined it closely.

"It looks a lot like Joe's house."

"Ya think so?"

Teddy grinned. "I like the way this little branch pokes out for the birds to sit on."

"Yeah, so do I."

Teddy ran a finger over the peak of the roof. "There's only one thing wrong with these houses."

Floyd frowned. "Yeah? What's that?"

"They're all just brown."

"They're made out of wood; what other color would they be?"

Teddy shrugged his thin shoulders. "You could paint 'em, make 'em all different colors. I bet Mrs. Culver could make 'em look real nice."

Floyd just grunted. "Well, this one's brown. You want it or not?"

Teddy nodded.

"You gonna take it with you, or you want I should set it over here until it's closer to Christmas?"

Teddy's enthusiasm slipped away. "I don't have any place to keep it. I'd better leave it here."

"No problem."

Teddy pulled out a small wad of crumpled-up one-dollar bills and paid for the birdhouse. Floyd cut the price to the cost of the wood, but didn't let on. He wrote Teddy a receipt for the money.

"Thanks, Mr. Culver."

"You're welcome, Teddy."

"Yoo-hoooo! Teddy, are you out here?"

"I'm here, Mrs. Culver!" The little boy raced off to where Doris stood in the open doorway. She looked pretty today, Floyd noticed. She'd begun to wear her hair loose once in a while, clipped back on the sides like she used to when they had first met.

A funny little stirring pulled low in his belly. He almost didn't recognize it. He chuckled. He and Doris hadn't shared a bed in years.

He thought how much he'd enjoyed the tea she had brought him, how, over the years, he had missed her soft, female chatter as they worked, how it always used to make him smile.

Floyd shook his head, thinking what a pitiful old fool he was to dream of the way it used to be.

❋ ❋ ❋

Joe had been taking Syl out a couple of nights a week since that Sunday in late October. At first, they carefully skirted any subject that had to do with the past and kept the conversation mostly in the present. Joe talked a lot about Teddy and how he was more and more determined to become the boy's foster father.

"I've hired a lawyer," he said as they drove toward the Dreyerville High School stadium. He was taking her to the Friday night Panthers' football game, the last one of the season. "Guy named Max Green. He's doing all the paperwork. He can't guarantee anything, of course, considering my record, but he thinks it's worth a try."

"I think hiring a lawyer's a good idea. Teddy's a wonderful little boy, and the two of you are perfect for each other. If there's any way to make it happen, you should try. And if there's anything I can do to help, you know I will."

Something moved across his features, but he kept his eyes straight ahead, firmly fixed on the road. "Thanks." He gave her a smile. "I hope you still like football."

They were meeting Charlie Murdock, Joe's best friend, and Charlie's wife, Betty Ann, at the stadium.

Syl had gone to school with Betty Ann and was looking forward to seeing her again after so many years.

"I used to be a real fan," Syl said, "back when you were playing." Both of them had gone to Dreyerville High, though Joe was older. He'd been the Panthers' star quarterback in his junior and senior years.

"You never knew who I was," she said with a smile, "but I knew you. All the girl's were in love with you."

Joe's eyes cut to hers. "How about you?"

Syl laughed. "Not then. I thought you were stuck-up and conceited. I didn't get hooked on you until we were in college." She fiddled with the hem of the red sweater she was wearing with a pair of black slacks—red and black, Panther colors. "You were amazing, Joe. I remember watching you run down the field. Nothing could stop you."

He chuckled. "Oh yeah? Seems to me like one of those big Warthog linebackers at the homecoming game stopped me cold. I had to be carried off the field."

Syl shivered. "I was so afraid when that happened," she said, silently remembering how she had worried that he might have been killed. She didn't tell him this now, but merely grinned at him. "Because I wasn't sure we could win the game without you."

His chest rumbled with laughter. "Coldhearted wench." Joe reached over and caught her hand, brought it to his lips. She felt the tingle all the way to her toes. "We did win, though, didn't we?" he asked.

"Because you came back on the field. Are you sorry you didn't go on playing? I know you dropped out not long after you started at Michigan. If you'd kept playing, you probably would have been drafted. You could have played professional ball."

Joe shook his head. "I'm not sorry . . . not about football. It's a game. I love watching, but I like what I'm doing now better. I like working for myself, being my own boss, setting my own goals."

"You always had such drive, so much energy. You wanted to make something of yourself . . . and you wanted a family."

He cast her a sideways glance. "I pretty much gave up that idea . . . until lately."

Syl gasped as Joe sharply turned the wheel and

pulled the car over to the side of the road. "I hate to do this, but I just can't wait any longer. Do you know how hard it's been for me not to kiss you?"

He popped his seatbelt and, before she could say a word, slid a hand behind her neck, pulled her toward him, and covered her mouth with his. The past came rushing back, the texture of his lips, the way they seemed to meld so perfectly with hers, the taste of him, the familiar scent of his cologne. The kiss wasn't soft and sweet. It was deep and burning, the kiss of a man who knew what he wanted.

"Nothing's changed for me, Syl," he said, kissing the side of her neck. "I thought it had, but I was wrong. I still want you. I still need you. I'm trying to be patient, to give us both time to see where this leads, but for me, I already know."

He kissed her again, softer this time, and she let him. Her insides were heating up, melting, and a sweet yearning bloomed in her chest.

"Let's skip the football game," he whispered, between soft, sensual kisses. "We were kids before. We didn't know what we were doing. We're adults now. We both have wants and needs. Let me make love to you, Syl."

Her breathing stalled. She eased back, pressed

her trembling hands against his chest, just hard enough to make him move away. Her heart was hammering, trying to pound its way through her ribs. "I—I'm not ready for that, Joe."

There must have been something in her voice, because he started frowning. "It isn't because of the cancer? Something that happened to you back then?"

"No, I . . . it isn't that." She looked up at him, tried to think if she should say it, decided that she might as well. "It's been years, Joe. If the right man had come along, it would have happened, but first I was sick, and then I was busy with my education, and then Aunt Bess fell ill. The timing was just never right, and now . . . well, I'm not quite ready to jump back in."

Joe was studying her in a different way than he had before, his eyes moving over her face. "Are you telling me . . . are you saying I'm it? I'm the only guy you've been with?"

She glanced away, embarrassed and feeling the way she had when she was a gawky young girl the guys always seemed to overlook. "I didn't plan it that way. Time just sort of slipped past."

Joe leaned toward her, framed her face between

his big hands, bent his head, and very softly kissed her. "God, I'm crazy about you. And I'm scared, Syl. Scared to death."

She pressed a kiss on his lips. "I'm scared, too, Joe."

On a shaky breath, she sat back in her seat, her heart still thumping wildly. "We'd better get going. Charlie and Betty Ann will be waiting. And we don't want to miss the kickoff."

"No," Joe said softly, his beautiful blue eyes on her face. "We wouldn't want to miss the kickoff."

CHAPTER NINE

<<<<<<<>>>>>>>

*I*t was another cold day, the temperature down in the thirties, an icy wind blowing through the barren trees. Floyd rubbed his hands together as he shoved open the door and stepped inside the back porch. He could smell something cooking in the kitchen, stew, he figured as he inhaled the succulent aroma. Doris made really good stew.

He moved toward the door leading into the kitchen, spotted her behind the wooden table, which was protected by sheets of newspaper. All her little paint pots sat on top: red, green, yellow, pink, every color he could think of. The entire house was filled with decorated plates and knickknacks, and those damned little figurines she gave away as presents no one really wanted.

Too damned bad she couldn't sell them. Maybe they'd have a little more room in the house.

"Floyd!" She turned, for the first time realizing he stood in the doorway. "I didn't hear you come in. I guess my mind was busy working." She set her brush down in front of the useless little plate she was painting, wiped her hands on the apron tied over her jeans, and came toward him.

"Are you hungry? I've got a pot of stew on the stove. I thought I'd make some biscuits to go with it, and we'd have it for supper, but there's plenty if—"

"I'm not hungry . . . not yet." He took the little wooden birdhouse he carried beneath his arm, walked over, and set it on the table.

"Teddy Sparks bought this. Wants to give it to Syl for Christmas."

"Well, isn't that nice. I hope you didn't charge him much for it."

"Just the cost of the wood." He ran a finger

over the gabled roof of the house. "Thing is, Teddy thinks it would look better painted. He thought you might do it for him."

Her eyes lit with interest. She'd always had pretty eyes. She walked over to examine the birdhouse. "You know, it might look real good painted some nice, bright colors. I could make the house yellow and the shutters dark green, something like that, maybe a bright blue roof."

"That sounds good." They talked a minute more, and then Floyd left the little birdhouse sitting on the table and headed for the door. He walked out of the warm, steamy kitchen, though he didn't really want to. He was pushing open the back porch door when he heard Doris's voice.

"Wait a minute, Floyd. Before you go back to the shop, why don't I make you a nice hot cup of tea?"

Floyd turned, a smile breaking over his face. "That'd be nice, Dorie. That'd be real nice on a cold day like this."

※ ※ ※

Syl sat across from Mary in the living room of Syl's apartment.

"So how's it going with Joe?" Mary asked, the question that hovered in both of their minds.

"We're still seeing each other at least three times a week. He's backed off a little, behaving like a real gentleman. He kisses me good night, but that's it. I guess he doesn't want to rush me. It's starting to drive me insane."

Mary laughed. Her dark, shoulder-length hair got caught in the collar of her turtleneck sweater, and she reached up and freed the strands. "Well, it's not like you two don't know each other well enough. Why don't you just jump him? That's what I finally had to do with Denny."

Syl smiled. "Actually, I've been thinking about it."

"So what's stopping you?"

She sighed. "I'm not sure. For starters, this whole thing with Teddy. Joe wants kids. Once I realized I would never be able to have them, I sort of put up this wall where children are concerned. I still like them, of course, but I'm always careful to keep a certain distance."

"Teddy's a really great kid."

"I know."

"I heard Joe's applied for some kind of guardianship or something."

Syl nodded. "He's got a petition in front of the court to become Teddy's foster parent. I think he'd adopt the boy if he could. With Joe's felony, it's against state law, but according to his lawyer, under certain circumstances, the judge can make an exception. I guess it doesn't happen very often."

"If you and Joe got married—"

Syl held up a hand. "I can't, Mary. I'm not ready to even think about marriage. That's one of the problems with Joe and me. If he asked me to marry him now, how would I ever know if it was me he wanted, or if he was just trying to maneuver the court?"

"I think Joe loves you. I don't think he ever really stopped."

"The timing's just not good, Mary."

Mary studied Syl's face. "You ran away once before, Syl, and came to regret it. You'd be a fool to do it again."

Syl said nothing. Joe had made a couple of comments about marriage, but she had purposely ignored them. He hadn't brought the subject up again, so it didn't really matter.

Making love to him, however, had nothing to do with marriage. At least not these days.

A knock sounded just then, and Mary jumped

up to answer the door. She checked the peephole first.

"It's Joe!"

"Well, let him in."

He walked in smiling, making Syl's breath catch, making her think how handsome he was and how much she wanted him to kiss her.

"Hi, Mary."

"Hi, Joe."

"Hello, Syl . . ." He held out the bundle wriggling in his arms. "I brought you something. You don't have to keep it if you don't want to."

She took a step toward him, saw that it was a puppy, black and white, with short, curly hair and a small, black button nose.

"Oh, Joe! He's adorable." She took the dog from his arms and cradled it in her own. The puppy looked up at her with big brown, liquid eyes that seemed to beg for a home.

"They're nothing but trouble," Mary warned. "But I'll take him if you don't want him."

"Not a chance!" Syl smiled up at Joe. "What kind of dog is it?"

"A male, some kind of terrier-poodle mix. He's definitely not purebred, so if that matters—"

"Not to me."

Joe reached over and scratched the puppy's ears. "Cute little devil, isn't he? They've got a lot of animals that need homes out at the pound. He's had his shots and been neutered and everything."

Mary flicked a glance at Joe. "Listen, you two dog lovers, I've got to run." She winked at Syl. "Remember what I said." And then she was gone, the door shut firmly behind her.

"So what'd she say?" Joe asked, taking the puppy from her arms and setting him down on the floor.

Why don't you just jump him? Syl hoped he wouldn't notice the color seeping into her cheeks. "Nothing. Just girl talk."

Joe turned back to the dog. "We're going to need some newspapers. He's already trained to use them. That's the first step, I guess. We can spread them on the kitchen floor."

Syl took care of the job while Joe went down to the car and got the dog food, water bowl, and bed he had bought.

"I've never had a dog," Syl said, grinning at the darling puppy sniffing around her feet.

"I remembered you saying way back when that

you'd always wanted one. I was hoping you'd like him."

"I love him. Thank you, Joe."

"So what are you going to name him?"

"I'll have to think about it." The puppy wandered around the house, checking out his new home, then climbed into his cozy little basket bed, curled up on the pillow in the bottom, and went to sleep. "Maybe I'll call him Lucky. It's lucky for me you gave him to me."

Joe chuckled. "It's luckier for him, and I hope you're still saying that next week." He gazed down at the dog. "Looks like he's already making himself at home. I envy the little guy . . . getting to sleep in your apartment."

Syl stared up at him, saw the warmth in his eyes, went up on her toes, and kissed him. It was a simple kiss, a thank-you. But the taste of him was heady, and when she parted her lips, the kiss turned deep and yearning, a thorough exploration unlike any of his kisses before.

Suddenly Syl had more than a thank-you in mind. She felt hot all over, as if she wanted to climb into his skin. When Joe tried to ease away, she slid her arms around his neck and wouldn't let him go.

"We're both adults," she whispered between soft, nibbling kisses, the words he'd said to her before. "We can do whatever we want."

Joe caught her shoulders, forcing her to look at him. She could read his hesitation, and his hope. "Are you sure, Syl?"

"I'm not . . . not really sure of anything right now. But I want this, Joe. I want you. Make love to me . . . please."

She didn't have to ask him twice. While the puppy snoozed in its basket, Joe swept her into his arms and carried her into the bedroom.

"I want to see you," he said, ignoring the curtains since the room was upstairs. "Watch your face when I'm inside you."

"Joe . . ." she whispered, reaching up to touch the hard line of his jaw, settling her mouth over his, and kissing him softly.

Joe helped her out of her clothes, and she helped him out of his, admiring his beautiful body, the muscles that were thicker now, the scars here and there that made him look even more masculine.

The wind blew outside, rattling the branches against the window panes, and the first flakes of snow began to fall. Winter would soon be upon

them. Christmas was not far away. As Syl welcomed
Joe into her body, felt the rightness of it, felt the
powerful connection she knew she would never feel
with another man, she thought that God had given
her an early present that blustery November day.

* * *

Thanksgiving came, but it wasn't the same as before.
The family Teddy was staying with, the Macks,
bought their Thanksgiving dinner down at King's
Supermarket. The food tasted okay, but he missed
his gramma's turkey with raisin and walnut stuffing
and her homemade punkin' pies.

Teddy got to stop by her house for a while that
Thursday afternoon, but the lady who lived with her
had bought the same dinner from King's he'd already eaten. He guessed no one cooked much, anymore.

He wondered what Joe got to eat. He wondered
if he'd had Thanksgiving with Miss Winters. Teddy
knew Joe liked Miss Winters a lot, and Teddy liked
her, too. She was always so nice to him, and when he
talked, it seemed she really listened.

He hadn't seen Joe for a while. The Macks
didn't think it was a good idea for an eight-year-old

to work in an auto shop, so he'd had to give up his after-school job. And they had told Joe not to stop by anymore.

Teddy wasn't sure why that was, but he overheard Mrs. Mack call Joe a *jailbird* in a nasty kind of way. The last time Teddy had seen his friend, Joe had said for Teddy to keep his hopes up, that he had hired a lawyer who was trying to find a way for Teddy to come and live with him. Every night before he went to bed, Teddy prayed it would happen.

Joe was his very best friend. Teddy had never had a father, but if he could pick one, he would pick Joe.

"Teddy! You get down here right now! You're going to be late for school!"

"Coming!" Teddy raced down the stairs into the kitchen, hoping Mrs. Mack wasn't scowling, but she was. He had only seen her smile a couple of times, maybe because she had two other kids and they never did anything she said. Teddy tried to do everything she wanted, but even when he did, she wasn't happy.

Tonight, he would pray even harder that the lawyer would fix it so he could go home with Joe.

* * *

A snowstorm hit the first week of December, but the snow melted away, leaving only a dry, brittle cold. Doris put the second coat of paint on Floyd's little wooden birdhouse with extra special care. It was for Teddy, and she wanted it to look just right. She added a couple of finishing touches and stepped back to survey the finished product.

As she had planned, the walls of the little house were yellow, but she'd decided to make the shutters a brighter shade of green. The roof she changed to red, which really set it off—or at least Doris thought so. When she heard Floyd wiping his feet outside the back porch, her stomach did a funny little twist. It was silly, but she wanted him to like what she had done.

"Thought I'd wind up a little early," he said. "Need to get some Christmas shopping done."

Doris nervously bit her lip, waiting for Floyd to notice the birdhouse. When she made no sound, his gaze swung to where she stood next to the table, and he spotted the bright yellow house.

He didn't say a word, just walked over and stood in front of it, studied it from several different angles. Doris held her breath.

"You know, that boy was right. Birdhouse looks a whole lot better all painted up this way."

She relaxed, gave him a bright, sunny smile. "I was hoping you'd like it."

Careful not to touch the still-wet paint, Floyd turned the birdhouse around to examine the back. "Teddy's gonna love it, and I think Syl will, too." He scratched the fringe of hair that rimmed his bald head. "You know, if you could find time to do a few more of these, we might try selling them down at the merc. I got a hunch they would go over real well."

Surprise widened her eyes. "You think so?"

"Yeah, I do."

"Well, you always did have a good head for business."

He glanced down at the toes of his work boots. "If you wanted . . . we could set up a table out in my shop. That way, you wouldn't have to put all your paints away every night when you got finished."

Her heart started thrumming, hammering with something that felt oddly like hope. "You'd let me work with you out in your shop?"

He shrugged his beefy shoulders. "We used to work together every day."

"Yes, we did."

"Used to be kind of fun."

Doris felt an unexpected burning behind her eyes. It took a moment to realize that it was the sting of tears. She turned away, dashed them off her cheeks with the hem of her apron, hoping Floyd wouldn't see.

She gave him another sunny smile. "Well, we could certainly give it a try . . . if you think you can find a table out there for me to use."

"I've got a couple I think will do. If it works out, we might want to get us a real heater in there . . . maybe one of those fancy jobs that's an air conditioner, too. That way, it wouldn't get too hot for you in the summer."

He was thinking that far ahead? That she would be with him out there in the summer? Doris said a silent, grateful prayer. "And we could still use the old stove," she added, "maybe put a tea kettle out there so we could make ourselves a nice cup when we felt like it."

Floyd smiled so wide that little crinkles formed beside his eyes. She couldn't remember the last time she had seen him smile that way. "Yeah, a little tea in the afternoon is always a good idea."

Doris's smile was equally bright.

It wasn't Christmas yet, but that didn't matter. Floyd had just given her the best Christmas present she had received in years.

CHAPTER TEN

❖❖❖❖❖❖❖❖❖❖❖❖❖❖

Syl dropped by the repair shop after work. Dr. Davis's office closed half an hour before the garage closed up, so she figured Joe would still be there. She thought she would see if he wanted to go get a pizza or something.

Syl smiled as she walked toward the glass front door beneath the new sign that read Dixon's Auto Repair. The name change was Bumper Murdock's early Christmas present to Joe, though Bumper would still be part owner until Joe's last payment, which was due next June.

Since that afternoon in her apartment, Joe had been spending most of his nights at her place, and it had been wonderful. He was everything she remembered him to be and so much more, a man now instead of a boy.

She was in love with him, she knew, and sometimes the fear arose. What if Joe's feelings for her weren't the same as hers were for him? What if his image of the girl she had been didn't match the woman she had become?

She tried to face her fears, which she handled okay most of the time. Today, they were nowhere in sight, and she just wanted to be with Joe.

She walked into the shop to find Bumper Murdock standing next to his son, Charlie. They were cookie-cutter images, two men built like fireplugs, except that Bumper had a roll around his middle that hung over his pants, and his dark brown hair was studded with silver.

"Hi, Bumper! Hi, Charlie!"

"Hey, Syl!" Charlie called back to her, and Bumper waved.

She glanced around, looking for Joe.

"He ain't here," Bumper said. "Had an appointment with that attorney he hired. Should be back, though, anytime soon."

"I think I'll wait."

She didn't have to wait long. Joe walked through the back door, and the instant she saw him, she knew something was wrong.

She hurried over, meeting him halfway across the shop. "What happened? Is it Teddy?"

Joe's jaw hardened. "The court turned down my petition. Said with my criminal record, it was too much of a risk."

"Oh, Joe." He walked into the waiting area and sank down heavily on the sofa. Syl followed him in, and so did Bumper and Charlie.

"That's a load of crap," Bumper said. "You were a kid back then. You're not like that now."

"The judge said if the court was to err, it had to be on the side of safety. They have to protect the kid."

It was a good argument, though in this case, the best place for Teddy was with Joe.

"So what are you gonna do?" Charlie asked.

"I don't know. The lawyer says we might be able to file an appeal, but even if we do——" He broke off, shook his head, swallowed. "I've got to tell Teddy. It isn't fair to keep his hopes up."

"Will the Macks let you see him?" Syl asked, her heart aching for Joe. Until this moment, she had secretly believed the court would grant him custody. Joe was meant to be a father. Knowing she could never give him the children he deserved was one of the reasons she had ended their engagement. Joe loved children, and he loved Teddy. There couldn't be a better man to become Teddy's father.

"I called Bill Mack. I told him the petition had been denied and asked if he would let me come over and talk to Teddy. Mack said it was okay."

He looked at her, and she could see the pain etched into his face. "God, Syl, what am I going to say to him? I let Teddy believe he could count on me, and now I'm letting him down."

"You tried, Joe. You did your best. That's all anyone can do."

He didn't answer her, just leaned over and gave her a brief kiss on the lips. "I need to go over there now. I'll call you when I'm finished."

"You want me to go with you?"

He shook his head. "Thanks, but I need to do this alone."

Syl understood. Her heart was hurting, aching for Joe. And for little Teddy. She watched Joe walk away, his broad shoulders slumped in a way she had rarely seen them.

She wished so much there was something she could do.

❋　❋　❋

Joe knocked on the door of the Macks' two-story brick home and waited for someone to answer. The house was in a middle-class neighborhood, the inside kept fairly clean. But there was something missing in this house, something Joe couldn't quite put a name to.

From what Joe had seen on his few brief visits, the two Mack kids had little respect for their parents. Which was maybe because the parents paid little attention to their kids. He wondered if they were doing the temporary foster home thing for the extra money or to prove to themselves they weren't really the rotten parents they seemed.

Whatever the reason, Joe hated that Teddy was there. Now that the petition had been denied, the court would find the boy a permanent placement. Joe prayed it was a better home than the one the Macks provided.

The odds weren't good. The system was over-crowded. Kids had to take what they could get. Joe tried not to think where Teddy might wind up.

The door swung open just then, and Teddy appeared in the opening. Joe's stomach knotted. "Hey, kid."

"Joe!" Teddy surprised him by running straight toward him, clamping his small arms around Joe's waist. Joe knelt in front of him, and the kid's arms went around his neck. Joe's chest squeezed. He had always wanted a son. Now it looked as if fate had put an end to that dream again.

Joe carried him over to the edge of the porch, and they sat down on one of the steps.

"Mr. Mack said you were coming over. I'm really glad to see you."

"Me, too, Teddy."

Joe asked him how he was doing in school, how he was getting along with Billy and Sissy, the two Mack kids, all the things an adult asks a child, anything to avoid the subject he had come to discuss. But time was ticking past, and occasionally, he saw Mrs. Mack peer out the window. He knew he wouldn't have much more time before they made Teddy come back inside the house.

"There's something we need to talk about, Teddy."

The boy looked up at him, his eyes dark and uncertain. "Coming to live with you?"

"I'm afraid that's not going to happen, son. You see, there's something I never told you, something that happened when I was younger. I got in a fight with a man, and when I hit him, he fell and hit his head. He died, Teddy, and I went to jail. That's the reason they won't let you live with me. They don't think I'd make a good father."

"Because of the man who died in the fight?"

Joe nodded. "I never meant for it to happen, but it was my punch that knocked him down. Refusing my request to become your guardian . . . that's just part of the price I have to pay for losing my temper."

"You don't lose your temper anymore."

"No, I don't. I learned a very hard lesson. But the law says a man with a criminal record can't be a foster parent."

Teddy's eyes glazed with tears. "Maybe if I told them what a good dad you would make, they'd change their minds."

"I wish they would, Teddy. God, I wish they

would. But I don't think that's going to happen."
He pulled the boy onto his lap and just held him.
Joe could feel the warmth of his small body, feel
him tremble with the effort to hold back his tears.

"So do I have to stay here with the Macks?"

"I'm not sure. The court will probably find you
a different home, someplace where you'll be happy."
Joe prayed he wasn't going to disappoint the boy
again.

"I'd be happy with you, Joe."

A lump formed in his throat. "I know you
would. I'd be happy with you, too, Teddy. But sometimes, God has other plans for us. Maybe he has a
family all picked out for you that is going to be just
perfect."

Teddy sniffled, buried his face in Joe's shoulder.
"I don't want another family. I want you, Joe."

Joe's eyes slid closed. "Don't cry, son. Everything's going to be all right."

"I'm not crying," Teddy said into the lapel of
Joe's wool coat. "Crying's for wimps, and I'm not a
wimp."

Joe almost smiled. "No, you're not." He eased
the boy a little away from him. Inside his chest, his
heart was squeezing, beating with heavy, painful

thuds. "You worked for me, didn't you? Right there at Murdock's Auto Repair. You were paid a wage, just like a full-grown man. I need you to be a man now, Teddy."

Teddy wiped the tears from his cheeks. His eyes looked deep and intense as he looked into Joe's face. "It's hard, Joe."

"I know, son. It's hard for me, too." He set the boy away from him, determined not to let the child see how upset he really was. He came to his feet and took hold of Teddy's hand. "I took your grandma's clock over to Mrs. Culver's. You can pick it up there when you go over to visit your grandma on Christmas Day."

Teddy just nodded. He had worked so hard for the money to buy the clock. He should have been proud and pleased. Instead, he no longer seemed to care.

Joe took a shaky breath. "Mrs. Mack probably has dinner almost ready. You better go in and wash your hands."

He glanced at the door as he said it, saw the robust woman standing in the open doorway, watching them with a look he couldn't read.

"You finished?" she asked.

Joe just nodded. Teddy reached out and caught his hand, gave it a last soft squeeze, and Joe's throat tightened until he couldn't speak.

"Bye, Joe."

He swallowed. "Bye, son."

"I love you, Joe."

He blinked against the burn of tears. "I love you, too, Teddy." Then he turned and strode down the front porch steps. As he climbed into his car and started the engine, Joe cast a last glance at the house. Teddy stood at the window, watching as he drove away.

✳ ✳ ✳

Joe stopped by Syl's apartment that night, but she could tell he didn't want to stay.

"I just . . . I'm not in a very good mood, baby. I'd be rotten company."

She didn't press him. She could see he was hurting. "Maybe you should talk to that attorney again. Maybe there's something else you can do."

"The attorney says I'd just be throwing good money after bad." He laughed darkly. "Imagine that. A lawyer who's not trying to get in your pocket."

"Still, you might be able to—"

"I have to let Teddy go, Syl. I don't want to give him any more false hope. He has to adjust, and the longer I stay in the picture the harder it's going to be for him to make a new life for himself."

Syl walked over and slid her arms around his neck. "Oh, Joe . . ."

He tightened his hold around her. "I feel so sorry for him, Syl. Teddy's never really had a family. Now . . . who knows where he'll end up."

Syl said nothing, just held on to him until he let her go.

"I'll call you tomorrow."

Syl watched him walk out the door, his body betraying his fatigue. It wasn't fair, she thought.

Not to Joe.

And especially not to Teddy.

CHAPTER ELEVEN

⬥⬥⬥⬥⬥⬥⬥⬥⬥⬥⬥⬥⬥⬥⬥⬥⬥⬥⬥⬥

*T*wo days passed, restless days for Syl. Work filled much of the time, but her mind remained on Joe. She was standing in the kitchen when Mary called. When she picked up the phone, it all came tumbling out.

"Oh, Mary, I feel so sorry for him. This whole thing with Teddy . . . it's killing him." Joe hadn't stayed with Syl since the night he had said good-bye to Teddy. He was too upset, too depressed.

Joe's heart was broken. Again.

This time, Syl wasn't going to let it happen. "There has to be something we can do."

"You're right," Mary said. "We can't just quit. Teddy needs Joe, and Joe needs Teddy. I'll talk to Denny. His dad's some fancy lawyer in Wicker County. Maybe he can figure out something."

"That'd be great, Mary. Call me back, will you?"

"You got it, honey."

Syl hung up, and within the hour, Mary phoned her back.

"Simon called—that's Denny's dad. He says we can ask for an appeal and request a hearing. If we can find the right people to testify in Joe's behalf and get a judge who's sympathetic, he might have a chance."

"Will you help me?"

"Don't be silly, of course I'll help. I've already got things rolling. Simon knows Joe. He's got an old Cadillac convertible he's in love with, a cherried-out nineteen fifty-nine—you know, the one with the big chrome fins? Apparently, Joe's the only guy he'll trust to work on it. Anyway, he said he'd file the paperwork for us—gratis. How's that for help?"

"Mary, you are the dearest friend a girl could ever have. Now all we have to do is find the right people to testify. We have to convince the judge that Joe Dixon is the *only* person suitable to become Teddy's dad."

* * *

The hearing was held three days before Christmas, in a small downstairs chamber in the courthouse. The lobby of the beautiful old granite building with its high, round dome had been painted during the Great Depression, the walls and ceilings covered with murals of men working in the fields around Dreyerville.

Inside the hearing room, Joe sat next to Simon Webster at a table in front of a low wooden railing that separated the bench from the seating area. Joe fiddled nervously with the pencil on top of his notepad.

"Take it easy," Webster said. He was a thin, sharp-featured, silver-haired man Joe could never have afforded to hire. "It isn't time to worry yet."

But Joe glanced over his shoulder just the same, praying to see Bumper and Charlie and their wives, and Denny and Mary Webster, all people who had agreed to testify in his behalf. Instead, Syl sat behind him just to his right, next to Floyd and Doris Culver. If he turned his head a little, he could see her.

She gave him a reassuring smile, but the muscles across his shoulders didn't loosen. Judge Halloran, a short, strictly no-nonsense older man with gray hair and horn-rimmed glasses, read the petition and opened the hearing to discussion.

The other side started first. "Your Honor, Social Services is convinced it can find the boy a permanent placement that would be far more suitable than the home Mr. Dixon could provide." This from a man named Linder, who was there representing the county's position. "Mr. Dixon is a convicted felon. That alone is enough to disqualify him as a foster parent. The state has rules against this sort of thing for a very good reason. The safer road is to stay within the rules."

"In a particular situation," Simon Webster argued, "sometimes the rules are not in the best interest of the child. That is the reason a hearing such as this one is available as an avenue of recourse. In the next few minutes, we plan to present reasons that will support Mr. Dixon's petition for the custody of Teddy Sparks."

Joe glanced toward the door. His heartbeat felt sluggish, his hopes dimming by the moment. He was sure he could count on his closest friends. Maybe something had happened to them. The roads were icy; maybe they'd had an accident.

Then the door shoved open, and his friends walked in, Bumper and Charlie and their wives, and Denny and Mary Webster.

One by one, Simon called each of them to the front of the room, where they talked about Joe and the sort of man he had always been, explaining that all through school, he'd been reliable and trustworthy. They talked about the man he had become since he had gotten out of prison and returned to Dreyerville.

"He's buying my shop," Bumper said. "Got the debt almost completely paid off. He's got plans to open a chain of repair shops, and he'll do it. Joe's got a big future ahead of him."

"Joe's always loved kids," Charlie said. "For years, he's helped me coach the junior football league after school."

Mary talked about her longtime friendship with Joe and Syl, and how sorry Joe was about what had happened that night in the bar.

"It never would have happened if he hadn't been so grief-stricken over losing Syl. Joe was never the kind of guy who would hurt someone on purpose. It was an accident. And Joe paid his debt to society for what he did that night."

Bumper's wife, Charlotte, and Charlie's wife, Betty Ann, told stories of Joe's helpfulness, how he always went the extra step with customers down at the shop. Doris and Floyd talked about Joe and said how much he cared for Teddy. They described how much Teddy's grandmother, Lottie Sparks, thought of Joe. Even Simon Webster spoke up for him, talking about how good Joe was with cars and how he never failed to do a good job. With this work ethic, the attorney said, Joe would be financially able to provide a solid home for Teddy.

Syl was the last to speak. A painful swell of emotion rose in Joe's chest as he watched her cross to the stand in her simple, dark green slacks and sweater and begin to talk about how good a father he would be.

"Joe's the sort of man who always sets a good example. He gave Teddy a part-time job so the boy could buy his grandmother a Christmas present. He knew he'd have to watch out for Teddy, make sure he was safe around all the equipment. He always made sure Teddy was out of harm's way whenever he was there in the shop. Joe loves that boy and Teddy loves him. Please, Your Honor, give Joe a chance to be a father and Teddy the home he deserves."

Watching her up there, Joe thought how much he loved her, how he had never really stopped. He thought how, no matter what happened, he wasn't letting her run from him again.

Judge Halloran looked at Joe and stood up, a solemn expression on his bulldog face. Joe's heart sank as the judge began to speak.

"I appreciate all of you coming here this afternoon. It's clear Joe Dixon has some very good friends, but we are talking about a young man's future here, not a matter to be taken lightly. There are a number of considerations beyond   "

A commotion stirred in the hallway, the sound of footfalls and murmurs out in the corridor. The door shoved open, and Joe caught a glimpse of tall, distinguished Reverend Gains before the entire entry filled to overflowing and a crowd of people pushed into the courtroom.

"We thought the hearing started at two," the reverend explained. "I hope we're not too late for the proceedings."

Joe could scarcely believe it. The hearing room

was suddenly packed with people, some of them he barely knew. The reverend's wife was there, along with their eldest son, Ben. He and Ben had played football together when Joe was the Panthers' quarterback. Tom McCabe was there, Joe's former parole officer. Jim Higgins, the nurse, and another nurse friend of Syl's from Dr. Davis's office.

Several of his customers were there, including Mrs. Murphy and Emma Kingsley and some of the ladies who ran the women's shelter. Joe saw Henry Tremont; Frank, Jr., and Mrs. Brenner from the bakery; Max Green, Joe's former attorney; and even Diane Ellison, the woman he had dated and almost married. Diane flashed him a smile and made the thumbs-up sign and joined the rest of the group in the room.

"Well, this is quite impressive," said the judge. "I presume all of you are here to support Mr. Dixon's petition for custody of Teddy Sparks."

"Yes, Your Honor," said Reverend Gains.

The judge surveyed the room, clearly recognizing a number of faces. "I'm sure all of you have something good to say about Mr. Dixon, so we'll just assume that and proceed." Heads turned, a few people grumbled. The judge ignored them.

"Before we were interrupted, I was about to say that it is clear Mr. Dixon has a number of friends here in Dreyerville, but there is a young man's future to consider. There are two more people I would like to hear from before we proceed any further." He rapped his gavel. "Bailiff, bring in the boy."

The crowd murmured; whispers were exchanged. Joe's chest squeezed as Teddy walked into the courtroom, holding on to a deputy's hand. He was scared, Joe could tell. His face looked pale as his dark eyes scanned the courtroom looking for Joe. Joe managed to smile when Teddy spotted him, and for an instant, the boy's face lit up.

Please, God . . . Joe silently prayed.

"All right, son," said the judge. "You know that Mr. Dixon has asked the court to set aside the rules and let you live with him."

Teddy nodded. "Yes, sir."

"I only have one question for you."

"Okay."

"What would make you happy?"

Teddy's gaze swung back to Joe. Hope shined in his eyes, and Joe prayed he wouldn't fail the child again.

"I want to live with Joe."

His eyes burned. The crowd rumbled its approval. Someone shouted, "Yes!"

"Thank you, Teddy. You may step down now." The bailiff led the boy back out of the courtroom, and the door closed behind them with an ominous clank.

Joe knew who would be last. His lawyer had told him just that morning that Elmira Mack had been asked to make a statement at the hearing. His stomach knotted. She didn't like him. She had made her feelings more than clear. Mrs. Mack's testimony would weigh heavily against him. Since she was part of the foster care system, the judge would pay extra attention to whatever she had to say.

"Is Mrs. Mack here?" the judge asked, his gaze searching the courtroom.

"Yes, Your Honor." The county attorney wore a smug look on his face.

Just then, the doors pushed open and the heavyset woman walked into the courtroom, broad hips swaying as she marched purposely down the aisle. She looked neither right nor left, just kept her attention straight ahead, a dour look on her face.

"Good afternoon, Elmira," the judge said as she settled her bulky frame in the chair next to the bench, and with the familiar address, any hope Joe had held disappeared.

"Good afternoon, Judge Halloran."

"Since the court is eager to settle this matter, we appreciate your time in coming down here this afternoon. If you would, Mrs. Mack, let us hear your opinion of what you think should be done with young Teddy Sparks."

A piercing look flashed toward Joe, one he was sure meant doom.

"Well, Judge, if I had been sitting in this box a few weeks ago, I would have told you the last person who should be allowed to foster Teddy was Joe Dixon. The man is a criminal, after all. He has no place being a father."

The knot in Joe's stomach tightened.

"I even thought that perhaps my husband and I should keep Teddy with us on a permanent basis."

Joe inwardly groaned.

"But there was a day a few weeks back that changed all that. I had never really noticed before, but that day, it all became clear. My father died when I was nine years old. He was the best father in the world, and he loved me very much. I've never stopped missing him." She fluttered a hand, bringing herself back on track. "At any rate, that last afternoon . . . as I watched Joe say good-bye to Teddy, I saw it and I knew. Joe looked at Teddy with the love of a father for his child. It was the way my father looked at me when I was a little girl." She summoned a watery smile, and it transformed her face. "In my opinion, Joe Dixon is the man who should raise Teddy Sparks."

The courtroom went wild, everyone talking at once, and the judge rapped the gavel.

"Quiet down—all of you! I won't have my courtroom disrupted."

Joe just sat there stunned. Mrs. Mack hefted her bulky frame out of the box and walked back down the aisle. When she paused briefly to squeeze his hand, he thought that maybe it was the holiday season, maybe the spirit of Christmas had touched Elmira Mack.

The crowd fell silent as she took a seat in the last row in the gallery. Joe held his breath.

The judge shuffled the papers in front of him, then looked up. "After such eloquent testimony from so many upstanding citizens of the community, I would be inclined to grant Mr. Dixon's request for custody. But unfortunately, there remains a problem I cannot simply overlook. As Mr. Dixon is a single individual—"

"He's getting married, Judge." Syl's voice spun him around in his seat. "Joe and I . . . we're getting married." She looked at him, and he could read her uncertainty, and her determination.

He had hinted at marriage a couple of times, but Syl had always changed the subject. He knew she loved him, just as he loved her. He'd just been giving her time to figure it out.

His heart filled with joy. He hoped she could see the love in his eyes as he dragged his gaze away from her and fixed his attention on the judge. "That's right, Judge Halloran." He couldn't stop smiling like a fool. "We're getting married just as soon as we can make the arrangements." He looked at Syl. "Maybe even this afternoon."

Syl grinned and nodded, and people started clapping. There were shouts of congratulations, stomping feet, laughter and whistles. Charlie reached over and slapped him on the shoulder.

The judge gave up a sigh of resignation. "Well, then, seeing as half the town of Dreyerville has come here in the belief that you are the best man for the job of raising this boy, I am going to make an exception to the rule. There will be official visits, of course, just to ensure that things are going along as they should. But assuming there are no unforeseen problems, I am going to grant your petition and place Teddy Sparks in your care—beginning as soon as you and Ms. Winters are married."

The courtroom erupted, and again the judge rapped madly. Everyone ignored him. Joe spotted Teddy running toward him and scooped him up in his arms. People were cheering and clapping, giving him their congratulations.

Joe searched the mob of people around him, frantically looking for Syl. Making his way through the crowd, Teddy clinging to his neck, he finally reached her and hauled her into his arms. "I love you, Syl. God, I love you so much."

"I love you, too." She wiped tears from her eyes. "Both of you." She kissed Teddy's cheek and smiled, and Teddy grinned.

"Are you gonna be my mom?"

"Yes, Teddy. We're going to be a family."

Joe's heart squeezed. *A family.* Eight years ago, he had lost Syl and the dreams they had shared. To-day, those dreams had all been given back to him.

As they made their way out of the courtroom and down the courthouse steps, friends and neighbors flowing out behind them, Joe ruffled Teddy's hair and reached for Syl's hand.

He thought of the incredible gift he had just been given, of the wrongs that had miraculously been righted and the gleaming future ahead of him. At the bottom of the courthouse steps, Joe looked up and whispered a silent prayer of thanks.

CHAPTER TWELVE

◇◇◇◇◇◇◇◇◇◇◇◇◇◇◇

Lottie sat in front of the Christmas tree. She didn't recall how the little tree had gotten there, but with all the lights and shiny ornaments, it certainly was pretty. And the little boy seemed to like it. She used to remember his name, but not anymore. She didn't tell him that, of course. He called her Gramma, so she figured they must be related, but she didn't really recall. She liked him, though. He was such a sweet little boy.

"Aren't you gonna open it, Gramma? Mrs. Culver helped me wrap it real pretty." He was there with his parents, a handsome black-haired man with lovely blue eyes and a woman with tawny brown hair and a pretty face. They were sitting on the sofa a few feet away, watching as the boy gave her his gift. She didn't remember either one of them, but they seemed like a very nice couple.

She smiled at the boy. "Thank you. . . . I love the silver paper and this beautiful red bow."

It was a big present and rather heavy, so the boy helped her take off the paper and open the box. "I paid for it myself, Gramma. I saved my money all summer."

She looked down at the box and lifted off the lid. Inside was an old Victorian gingerbread clock. Something stirred inside her, a memory from the past. Her mother cooking in the kitchen, steam rising from a pot boiling on the stove. There were cookies in the oven. The aroma of chocolate filled the air, and she remembered licking the batter off the spoon her mother handed her.

"Do you like it, Gramma?"

She looked back down at the clock. There was one just like it in her family's kitchen when she was a little girl. She hadn't remembered that for so long . . . so very long. She didn't remember very much anymore, but that day in the kitchen with her mother . . .

She turned to the boy. "It's wonderful. It makes me remember nice things. Thank you very much."

She gazed at the clock. She must have been staring at it for quite some time, because the woman—Lottie kept forgetting her name—came in and said it was time for her nap. The house was empty except for the two of them. It seemed as though someone had been there earlier, but maybe she was wrong.

She looked at the clock sitting in front of her and caught sight of the lighted tree. It was Christmas. It had been Christmas that day in her mother's kitchen. Lottie remembered that day . . . so very long ago.

Epilogue

And so it was that Christmas in 1994 that set the stage for the man I became. As I walk across the platform and accept my college diploma, I think of my grandmother, Lottie Sparks, and the clock that led me to the people who became my family, the people I love. My grandmother is no longer living, but I will never forget her or the things she taught me.

My name is Theodore Dixon now, but everyone still calls me Teddy. My mother and father have been married fourteen years, and every day, I'm grateful they were willing to open their hearts and give me a loving home.

I have three brothers and sisters, all of us adopted. Of course, I like to think I'm the favorite, since I was the first, but I know Randy, Jimmy, and Amy are loved as much as I am.

We're a family, no matter where we came from, and for all of us, our favorite holiday is Christmas.

In the heat of this bright summer day, the holidays seem distant, but soon the leaves will begin to fall and snow will be on its way. Christmas will come, a time of celebration, joy, and grateful prayers.

A time I give thanks for the miracle I was blessed with that day at the courthouse so many years ago.

Dear Readers,

I hope you enjoyed *The Christmas Clock*. As I considered how best to tell this story, setting it a few years back in time to a softer, less hectic era seemed somehow right. The inspiration for Dreyerville came from the small Michigan town of Ionia. With a population of less than 10,000 at the time the book took place, it is a lovely little village filled with turn-of-the-century homes, steepled churches, and a main street lined with old-fashioned street lamps and nineteenth-century businesses that look just as they did back then.

Of course I took liberties with the businesses themselves, but anyone who has read *The Christmas Clock* will see a lot of Ionia in Dreyerville.

If you decide you would like to revisit the town, I hope you'll watch for *A Song For My Mother*. You'll meet a few more of the locals and catch up with a few old friends. It's out before Mother's Day in Spring 2011.

Till, then happy reading and all best wishes,

Kat

Q & A WITH KAT MARTIN, AUTHOR OF
The Christmas Clock

The Christmas Clock is a departure from your usual writing. What inspired you to write this story?

My husband's mother, a wonderful lady, had Alzheimer's disease. I saw firsthand what a terrible disease it was. Watching her slip away became the kernel of an idea for this story.

What meaning does Christmas have for you? What are some of your family's traditions?

We always have a real Christmas tree. There is something about the scent of pine and candles. We cook a turkey and have the whole family over on Christmas Day and also plan something special on Christmas Eve.

Is there a clock in your life that has special meaning to you?

My mother collected antique clocks. They all had special meaning for her. Though she is no longer with us, I felt that the clock in the story could have a similar meaning for Lottie.

What glimpses of Kat Martin are there in this book?

Well, I love Christmas and to me it's a very special time of year. I am a true romantic and I love happy endings. You will find one in every one of my books.

The book begins and ends with an adult Teddy recalling a series of significant events that forever impacted his life and the lives of those around him. Can you describe a time in your life when all the pieces fell into place at the right time?

I would say that meeting my husband was the significant event that changed my life. Because of him I started writing. With his encouragement, I've continued a career that I feel is my life's calling.

One theme throughout The Christmas Clock *is returning—Sylvia Winters returns to her hometown, Joe Dixon returns after prison, they both return to college, Sylvia and Joe return to each other, as do the Culvers. What significance does the idea of returning have to you?*

Sometimes returning to a place completes the circle. Unfinished problems are resolved. Unfinished relationships are made whole. Returning can be a healing process.

Home also serves as a significant theme throughout the book. Syl moves home. Teddy needs a home. Joe and Syl want to create a home. Even the Culvers find each other by creating homes for birds. What does home mean to you?

Home is a place that lives inside us! A place where we can feel safe, somewhere we feel connected to our past. Some of us go home, some of us don't, but the notion of home stays with us throughout our lives.

A third theme involves the loss of significant relationships— grandparent, parent, child, lover, even the loss of self through disease and prison. How have you learned to deal with loss?

People deal with loss in different ways. My way has always been to look forward, to think of the future, rather than dwell in the past. I would hope that is what my lost loved ones would want me to do.

The Culvers, who have been married for many years, live estranged lives. In your opinion, what does it take to keep a marriage healthy, happy and fulfilled?

Spending time together. Being able to forgive each other. We are all bound to say the wrong thing, do the wrong thing at one time or another. Love each other unconditionally. That is the key.

What unique challenges did you encounter in writing The Christmas Clock?

I did a great deal of research on Michigan, cervical cancer and, of course, Alzheimer's disease. Putting it all together was also a challenge.

How does writing fulfill you?

It's like putting puzzle pieces together. Once the story is completed, there is a terrific feeling of satisfaction. It is even more gratifying when readers enjoy the book.

DISCUSSION QUESTIONS FOR

The Christmas Clock

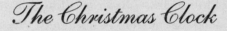

I. Sylvia Winters returns to Dreyerville, Michigan, eight years after surviving cervical cancer and leaving her fiancé. She had only visited the small town once when her alcoholic mother died. Why do you think Sylvia returned home? What did the small town offer her? Would you have returned? What does "home" mean to you?

2. Abandoned, broken-hearted and confused, Joe Dixon drops out of college and begins drinking heavily after Sylvia Winters leaves. After serving time in prison, he returns to Dreyerville to help run a business. How did prison affect Joe and his life? Discuss a time when you made an impulsive decision that later impacted your life.

3. The story opens and closes with an adult Teddy Sparks Dixon recalling the series of events that led him to his family. What significant events in your life have helped you reach a goal, achieve a dream, or influenced your life's path?

4. Doris Culver believes that "love . . . was for fools and dreamers, and she never allowed herself to succumb to its lure again." She and her husband, Floyd, live barren lives, emotionally and physically. They each find joy in their own hobbies, but not with each other. Why did this happen with Doris and Floyd? Why does this happen to real-life couples? Doris and Floyd managed to find each other again. What does it take to rekindle love?

5. Lottie Sparks keeps her diagnosis of Alzheimer's disease from her friends and Teddy. Sylvia Winters keeps her diagnosis of cervical cancer from Joe. Why was keeping medical secrets from loved ones a theme in the book? If you have had a serious medical situation, when did you tell your family and friends? Looking back, would you have handled the situation differently?

6. Lottie Sparks' Alzheimer's disease impacts many characters and circumstances in the book. According to the Mayo Clinic, about 5 percent of people between the ages of 65 and 74 have Alzheimer's disease, while nearly half the people over the age of 85 have Alzheimer's. As our society ages, more families will have to cope with the debilitating disease. What would you do if you recognized possible symptoms in a neighbor or relative? How would you help care for a family member struck with the disease? How would you want to be cared for if you developed the disease?

7. When Joe sees Syl at the grocery store, he's both angry with her and still attracted to her.

How would you feel about seeing a long-lost love who bitterly hurt you? How would you respond to that person?

8. Syl eventually goes to Joe's apartment to tell him the truth about why she left. Would you have done the same? Why or why not? Joe initially feels even more betrayed that Syl hadn't trusted him enough to tell him about the cancer at the time. Would you have been able to forgive a partner who lied to protect you? Would you be able to allow yourself to fall in love with someone who'd betrayed you? What would it take to reconcile?

9. All the characters in *The Christmas Clock* suffered the loss of significant relationships—Syl lost her mother and Joe, Teddy lost his parents and his grandmother, Joe lost Syl, Lottie lost her daughter and Teddy, and the Culvers lost their love for each other. How did these losses impact the characters and their stories? How has losing a parent, child, partner or other close relationship affected you and your life?

10. In the end, broken relationships are healed and dreams are fulfilled. What relationships have been healed in your life? Which ones still need healing? Elmira Meeks surprises everyone by supporting Joe. Who has surprised you in your life with caring, kindness, or support? How have relationships—whether close or casual—helped you fulfill your personal dreams?

Following is an excerpt from the
forthcoming novel

The Perfect Love Song:
A Holiday Story

BY

PATTI CALLAHAN HENRY

Published by Vanguard Press
Available October 2010

CHAPTER ONE

*The truth inside the story is
what the storyteller aims for . . .*
—Maeve Mahoney to Kara Larson

Jimmy Sullivan—God bless his soul—wrote the perfect Christmas song. Now, I'm not the only one who says this, so don't go thinking this is just my opinion. This was so perfect a song that it almost ruined him.

When Jimmy wrote this song it was his first holiday season with Charlotte. Well, not technically his first, but when it comes to storytelling I'm not really sure if the word "technically" should enter our minds or hearts. Pure love formed this song. Of course, this is where the best stories, melodies, and lyrics are born: love. You might not believe that a mere song can change a life, but I'm here to tell you that it can and it did.

• • •

It was Thanksgiving morning when the Unknown Souls band tour bus pulled up to the Larson family house. Brothers Jack and Jimmy Sullivan were asleep in the backseat, exhausted after their Savannah concert the previous night. It was a balmy coastal morning in Palmetto Pointe, South Carolina, the air infused with the rain of the past two weeks. The palms bent low in submission from the constant beating of wind and rain, the ground damp with the sweet smell of earth, sea, and life combined—an aroma of their childhood.

Jack woke first and shook Jimmy. "We're here, bro, and you're staying for the day. No arguments."

Now, normally Jimmy wouldn't want to be staying for this family thing; he'd rather hang out with the band. The poor boy just wasn't much on domestic events (I'll tell you more about that soon), even if the family belonged to his brother's girlfriend, Kara, who was his childhood next-door neighbor. But the one thing that can change a man's mind made Jimmy stay—the love of a woman. Kara's best friend, Charlotte, would be here today, and Jimmy was falling in love with her. He'd known Charlotte briefly as a child, and he denied this blooming love to his brother and anyone who would listen. No one believed him. Love like that is obvious to everyone within a heart's distance.

"We have to be on the road by 9:00 a.m. for the concert in Nashville," Isabelle, one of the backup singers, called from the back of the bus, her voice still as brittle and hard as it had been since Jack admitted his love for Kara. She couldn't help it—love denied sometimes hardens the heart. It doesn't have to be this way, and Isabelle's heart will soften with time.

Jack and Jimmy stood at the bus door when Porter Larson, Kara's dad, appeared and poked his head into the bus. He hugged Jack. Now, this right here was a Thanksgiving miracle because Mr. Larson was none too keen on Kara's breaking up with Mr. Hotshot Golfer to hook up with an old neighbor who was now in a country band. But Porter's smile and hug sang of a changed heart.

"Hello there!" Porter hollered, uncomfortable

around the band, but wanting to be friendly. "What's everyone doing for Thanksgiving?" He glanced around the bus.

Isabelle answered for the group. "Happy Thanksgiving to you, Mr. Larson. I think we're headed to the beach for the afternoon. We have a concert tomorrow, so . . . "

"Oh, no, you don't," Porter said. "You're coming to spend the day with us."

Luke, the band director, stood up and walked toward the front of the bus. "We're fine, Mr. Larson. You've got your hands full with the Sullivan boys here."

"Please," Porter said. "We'd love it and we have plenty of food. Kara and Charlotte have been cooking for days."

The band members shrugged and laughed (except for Isabelle). Harry, the drummer, stood, holding drumsticks in his hand as he always did. He played the air when he couldn't play the drums. "I'm betting Kara Larson's turkey is better than our sub sandwiches."

The house was bright and warm that morning as the bedraggled group followed Mr. Larson to the living room. Jimmy burst through the door, hugging and greeting the entire family. The smell of cinnamon, pine, and something cooking in the back of the house filled Jimmy with a longing for things lost and never had. He wondered how he, so undeserving, could be blessed enough to walk into this house, into this family, and toward the open arms of Charlotte Carrington.

Then the noise began. Kara's sister and brother-in-law, Deidre and Bill, came through the front door at the same time, hollering for help with the food and case of wine. Then came Kara's brother, Brian.

The house filled with noise in that gorgeous way of family, of laughter and private jokes. The band crowded the living room, men and women with guitars and drumsticks looking misplaced on the prissy antique furniture of Mr. Larson's living room, which looked exactly the same as the day his wife, Margarite, passed away, twenty years ago. Damask curtains fell to the floor where Isabelle sat cross-legged, and she began to tell the stories, the ones about Jimmy and his antics on the road. She is good at this, and laughter rang out like the sound of hope as she told the story about Jimmy's hiring a girl to run up on stage and dance around Jack, trying to rope him with a lasso as he sang the Toby Keith song "Shoulda Been a Cowboy."

Jack shook his head. "I'm telling you, I almost killed him, but what would we do without Jimmy's jokes on tour? I think sometimes they save us from insanity, even when we beg him to stop." The combined voices and warm food, the cold wine and deep laughter, filled the room.

Sometimes Thanksgiving Day is all it should be in a family, in a home. That day inside the Larson home was one of those. In the simple and undeserved way of love, hearts mended and relationships were stitched together over food, twinkling lights, bad jokes, laughter, and melancholy memories. They talked about Maeve Mahoney, the Irish woman Kara believes brought her back to Jack. They spoke of Margarite and how both Margarite and Maeve seemed to be present in all that was said and done that day. They spoke of Jack and Jimmy's sweet mother, Andrea, now in California. Even Isabelle's mouth broke into a smile that didn't leave her face for the remainder of the day.

Charlotte brought her mother, Rosie, and soon the house filled with a light that Jimmy believed only he could see. He watched Charlotte with her wide smile and long blonde curls, Charlotte with her sweet laugh, tender touch and gentle words. Families had never been a safe place for Jimmy, and he'd believed they never would be, like growing up in a war-torn country and then believing that all lands are the same. But here he was beginning to relax into the rhythm of a new place where Charlotte inhabited not only the Lowcountry, but also his heart.

• • •

Charlotte and Jimmy met as all the best lovers do—when they weren't looking for love, when they were too busy to notice they'd stumbled upon treasure. They were brought back together when Kara and Jack reunited.

Now, Kara and Jack's love story has been told, but it is so beautiful that I love to tell it again and again, recalling the events with long, beautiful sighs.

You see, Jack and Kara were childhood sweethearts, yet were separated when they were twelve years old. You can split a boy and girl apart, but here's what you can't do: take the love out of their hearts. No, you just can't. Love is alive inside a heart the same way blood moves inside a body—running and thrumming through every cell and unseen thing that make us who we are.

The story of how they ended up together is

much more complicated than just finding one another again. It had been in May of the previous year, and sweet Kara was engaged to the wrong man. Not a bad man. No, not that. Just wrong for her. Now, poor Kara had lost her mother when she was nine, and her daddy was a strict man who just wanted the best for his daughter and thought that her famous fiancé was the best thing for her. She wanted to please her daddy. Who doesn't? This is built into the human soul like a building block.

Kara was working for the PGA Tour, not only a grand job in her father's eyes but a vocation that allowed her to meet Peyton Ellers, who was and is a star on the tour. Peyton was all those things a girl like Kara, a good girl trying to do all the right things at the right time, would have looked for and loved. And sometimes when everything looks just right, we think it is just right when it merely looks that way. We have to search a little deeper.

About this time in Kara's very perfect life entered this batty old lady named Maeve Mahoney. Well, to be precise, Kara entered Maeve's life when Kara walked through the front doors of the Verandah Nursing Home and into Maeve's room, stating, "I'm here to spend some time with you."

You see, although Kara was "spending time" with Maeve, these times were "volunteer" hours mandated by the Service League, hours that Kara needed to fulfill in order to avoid being fined. Kara showed up with a pleasant-enough attitude, but yes, she was assigned to spend time with this woman. Maeve immediately saw that Kara was leafing through a wedding magazine, and that she was harried, hurried, and preoccupied, so Maeve began to speak about true love, narrating first-love stories. Now, let me tell you, Kara merely and only tolerated this woman's ramblings at first, believing that Maeve was crazy and had confused life and love and Ireland and Scaboro into a mishmash of memories. But soon it became evident that Maeve was telling a love story, one that sounded a lot like the tale of the Claddagh ring, a story clouded in myth and legend with a little blarney thrown in for good measure. Is there any better kind of story?

The Claddagh ring is that common symbol we all know—two hands circling a crowned heart—worn by lovers and friends all over the world. A symbol of love and fidelity. The tale goes something like this: There was a man from Claddagh, Ireland, Richard Joyce. In the seventeenth century he left the woman he loved and sailed to the West Indies for a job, but alas, on the way, he was kidnapped by Moorish pirates and sold into slavery. Eventually, he apprenticed to a goldsmith in Algiers, where he fashioned and crafted the first Claddagh ring of gold, as a gift for the woman he loved back home, the woman he knew he would return to one day. When Richard was finally freed, he came home and discovered that his true love had waited; he gave her the ring, and they wed. Ah, the perfect love story, right?

Well, soon the myth of Richard Joyce and Maeve's own love story about a man also named Richard began to weave into one love story until Kara was quite sure that Maeve was mixing up life and myth, confusing fact and story—Kara not yet knowing that all those can and often do combine into the most beautiful of all things: truth.

In broken fragments, Maeve told Kara of her own love, her own Richard, a man Maeve loved and lost and searched for and never found, a man who broke her heart and a man for whom she wished she'd had the tenacity and heart to have waited. This tender story opened Kara's heart to what she had known all along: She still loved Jack Sullivan. Yet and still, Kara did not believe that Maeve's story was "real," as the details were far too close to the myth of the Claddagh ring.

During these days that Kara came to love Maeve and her legends and tales, she also came to realize that in many ways Maeve was also telling Kara's story, asking Kara to look into her own heart to find the truth of her life. Soon Kara understood the lessons inside Maeve's narrative, and it was then and only then that Kara began to listen to the hints and proddings of her own heart. And it was then that she went to look for Jack Sullivan.

Kara spent hours listening to Maeve, pondering the questions Maeve asked her, questions like: "If you knew he'd return, would you wait for him?" and "Who was your first love?" Yet Kara still did not believe Richard was a real man until she found historical documents about the man Maeve had once loved, Richard O'Leary. Only then had Kara finally believed in the truth.

Who can tell the exact moment when a woman or man believes in something? Who can tell the exact moment when someone falls in love? Same thing. Believing. Love. Same thing.

So, you see, both Maeve's myth and truth

brought Jack and Kara back together. And sometimes, oh, sometimes, it is this kind of love that also changes everything else in their world. Which this love did do.

• • •

I'm sorry—I know I digressed. Let me get back to how Jimmy and Charlotte came together because that is what this story of the song is all about. Well, really it's all about undeserved love, but the story of the song and undeserved love are one and the same. You'll see.

Charlotte is Kara's best friend and has been since second grade. Kara and Charlotte found each other during that time in life when a mother's death leaves a hollowed-out hole in the soul. Their common interest in art drew them together, although they could not have understood at that young age what brought them together; they merely felt that their hearts called out for one another in an immediate way.

The way an author wraps words around life to explain and describe, so Kara uses her camera and Charlotte her designs, both making sense of life through artistic expressions. And except for their

deep love for one another, that is where their similar-
ities end. Kara is organized and precise, whereas
Charlotte is scattered and free-spirited; Kara's hair is
a deep brown, straight and controlled, whereas Charlotte's loose blonde curls fall free and wild no matter
what she tries to do with them. Kara's cottage is a
home on the water, filled with white furniture and
clean lines; Charlotte's apartment overflows with
swatches of fabric, paint chips, and poster boards,
toppling with ideas. Kara's books are in painted
bookcases lined up alphabetically by author, Charlotte's books arranged in no order other than color
and style.

Sometimes friendships form in the long flow of
days, like a river carving a new path through the land,
and yet other friendships are wrought together like
iron to iron in a single moment. The day of Kara's
mother's funeral, the adults, engulfed in their own
grief, had left the girls alone for most of the day. Together they'd hidden under the branches and tangled
roots of the old magnolia tree in the front yard.
Curled into one another with ham sandwiches
wrapped in flowered napkins, chocolate chip cookies
melting in their pockets, they'd eaten, whispering
stories of ghosts and angels, of where Margarite

Larson was at that moment. Had she been able to talk to Jesus? After the devastation of chemotherapy, had all her hair grown back when they gave her a halo? They'd then fallen asleep to the lullaby of the wind, of the voices of adults wafting toward them, but never fully reaching their ears.

When the darkness settled into the crevices of the yard, and when the day they buried Kara's mother finally ended, no one could find the best friends. Adults called their names, searched the neighbors' homes and yards. Yet it was Jack who discovered them. It was Jack who knew where they'd gone and why. He slipped under the branches and woke them, knowing in that way that children know that the friends would not want anyone to see where they'd been. Together the three of them walked into the dark night, where Charlotte looked up to the brightest stars and said, "Do you think she can see us through those holes in the sky?"

"Those aren't holes, Charlotte," Kara said in a voice that was now more grown-up than it had been even a day before, death somehow transforming a child into an adult.

Charlotte stopped, grabbed her best friend's hand. "Tonight they can be holes in the sky, right?"

Kara stood for the longest time staring up into the sky and even past the sky, farther and deeper, until she returned her gaze to Charlotte and Jack. "Yes, well, yes, they could be holes if we wanted them to be."

And together the three friends slipped quietly into the house where the friendships that last forever tie their first knots into the soul. You see, there are moments, small and momentary, fleeting but defining, and Kara had decided right there, in that moment, on that night, that even with her mother gone, mystery still remained; with her best friend and Jack at her side, magic yet lingered.

And Jimmy, well, he is Jack's brother. And let me tell you something, these boys have suffered in this world. Oh, my heart aches to think of their hurt. The pain a father can inflict on his son is almost the worst pain there is. And love heals even that. Yes, love heals the worst of all wounds. It is why Love is here in this world, why Love came unasked and undeserved.

So Jimmy and Charlotte were, as I said, forced together by circumstance, yet their hearts came together with something altogether different from mere situation. Which brings me back to the song.

• • •

Jimmy sat in the Larson living room, and if love can be overwhelming (which, of course, it can be or it isn't love), it was at that moment. And this is what he thought when Charlotte walked across the room:

> *I cannot find or define the moment you entered*
>   *my heart.*
> *When you entered and turned a light on in the*
>   *deepest part.*

Lyrics began to form in his mind as Jimmy grabbed a notepad and pen from the kitchen, and then slipped away quietly to the footbridge at the end of the road. He glanced backward at the house next door to the Larsons', the house where he had grown up and left at sixteen years old. Yes, Jack and Jimmy grew up next door to Kara. The tangled memories often left Jimmy dizzy. How should he feel about a place where he had once had a mother as loving as his, a place that had allowed him to live in this quaint, coastal town, and yet a home where an abusive and drunk father hung like a noxious, poisonous cloud over their lives?

Only a woman like Charlotte could get him to return to this land and world to celebrate a holiday. Jimmy sat in the damp, quiet afternoon, the cicadas clicking the notes of the music, the river carrying lyrics, the air itself drenched with the song for Charlotte, the song about undeserved love entering a heart to change it forever. When he'd finished, he slipped the song into his back pocket and returned to the house, to Charlotte.

Now, Jimmy didn't want to sing this song to Charlotte until Christmas Day (it would be the only present he could afford). He wanted to polish and fix the words, make it perfect, although it had arrived complete as it was—the song his secret.

When he returned to the house Charlotte stood in the kitchen washing dishes with Kara. There Charlotte stood with her blonde curls loose and tangled, the smell of soap and spice mixed into the warm kitchen, her voice soft and full. He came up behind her, kissed her ear.

She turned to his smile. "Where have you been?"

"I just needed some fresh air."

"We are all just too, too much sometimes, aren't we?" she asked, lifting her gloved and soapy hand.

"Yes," he said. "Sometimes." He laughed. I love when this man laughs because for so many years he was unable.

"I'm sorry," she said. "I know holidays are . . . not your favorite."

"No, not my favorite," he said. "But you are."

She shook her head. "Oh, Jimmy." She rested her head on his shoulder and sighed.

It is a blessed thing when a woman loves a man this way. It is where healing begins in a heart. Ah, but more must happen, because this was only the beginning.